"I don't want   but I'm not sure that I can take care of a baby," Ben said.

Sara grabbed Ben's shirtsleeve. "You're not thinking of sending him away, are you? After all, they left the baby with you. You can't send little Tyler away without even trying to help him."

The doctor came in, smiled at them, then went right to Tyler's bed. "Well, well, Reverend. Let's have a look at your little bundle of joy."

Ben glanced at his friend, then back to the red-haired, obviously determined woman flashing green fire at him. "I just don't know..."

"I'll help you with Tyler," she offered. "You should keep him here, surrounded by people who care, until we can decide what to do."

Ben could only nod. Sara certainly seemed determined to keep the baby nearby, but he wasn't so sure. But God didn't always send His answers in the easiest, most convenient packages. Sometimes they came in the form of an adorable baby and a red-haired woman with attitude.

Books by Lenora Worth

Love Inspired

The Wedding Quilt #12
Logan's Child #26
I'll Be Home for Christmas #44
Wedding at Wildwood #53
His Brother's Wife #82
Ben's Bundle of Joy #99

LENORA WORTH

grew up in a small Georgia town and decided in the fourth grade that she wanted to be a writer. But first she married her high school sweetheart, then moved to Atlanta, Georgia. Taking care of their baby daughter at home while her husband worked at night, Lenora discovered the world of romance novels and knew that's what she wanted to write. And so she began.

A few years later, the family settled in Shreveport, Louisiana, where Lenora continued to write while working as a marketing assistant. After the birth of her second child, a boy, she decided to pursue her dream full-time. In 1993 Lenora's hard work and determination finally paid off with that first sale.

"I never gave up, and I believe my faith in God helped get me through the rough times when I doubted myself," Lenora says. "Each time I start a new book, I say a prayer, asking God to give me the strength and direction to put the words to paper. That's why I'm so thrilled to be a part of Steeple Hill's Love Inspired line, where I can combine my faith in God with my love of romance. It's the best combination."

Ben's Bundle of Joy
Lenora Worth

Published by Steeple Hill Books™

Special thanks and acknowledgment are given to Lenora Worth for her contribution to the Fairweather Miniseries.

STEEPLE HILL BOOKS

Steeple Hill™

ISBN 0-373-87105-8

BEN'S BUNDLE OF JOY

Copyright © 2000 by Steeple Hill Books, Fribourg, Switzerland

For you were once darkness, but you are light in the Lord. Walk as children of the light.

—Ephesians 5:8

To Anne Canadeo, with gratitude and appreciation

Chapter One

Deep within the still, peaceful confines of the old church, he thought he heard a baby's soft cry. Glancing up, Reverend Ben Hunter decided he must be imagining things. He was alone in the church, alone with the brilliance of stained-glass windows on a crisp, sunny October morning, alone with his own unvoiced thoughts and unanswered prayers. It was too early in the day and way too quiet for any of his overly protective members to be paying a visit to the sanctuary of The Old First Church of Fairweather, Minnesota.

At least he hoped so.

Ben liked being alone. Not that he minded having to deal with his congregation and their joys and concerns on a daily basis, but he craved the peace and solitude of his private early-morning devotionals here in the church that he'd called home for the past three years. But was this really his home? Would it ever be?

He didn't get a chance to ponder that particular prayer request. The cry came again, this time impatient and almost angry, but still soft, like the mewling of a kitten.

Lifting his athletic frame off the aged pine pew in the middle of the small church, Ben shook his head as he followed the sound toward the back. "Not another kitten. Emma, Emma, when will you stop trying to push pets off on me?"

He knew the church secretary, Emma Fulton, meant well. Emma was a social butterfly. She liked being the center of attention, and she liked having people and pets around all the time. So, naturally she thought Ben needed the same in his life—for companionship. Which meant she was constantly trying to fix him up with either blind dates or abandoned animals. Ben didn't know which was worse—the setups never panned out because he usually never heard from the ladies again, and because he couldn't turn the animals away, he was slowly collecting a small zoo. At least the animals took a liking to him, even if none of the single women in town did.

"I can't take any more strays, Emma," he said, his voice echoing over the cream-colored walls and vaulted, beamed ceiling of the antique church. He half expected the plump secretary to jump out from behind a pew, singing one of her favorite hymns. As he reached the back of the church, though, Ben stopped and stared into the sturdy cardboard box someone had left on the pew. This was no ordinary stray.

This one was human. A baby. A tiny newborn baby lay kicking and whining in the box, mounds of blankets encasing the ruddy little body.

"Well, hello there," Ben said, glancing around to see if anyone would come out and lay claim to the infant. "How did you get here, little one?"

This time the baby's cry grew louder, more demanding. Not sure what to do, Ben reached down and lifted the infant out of the box, careful to keep it wrapped in the protective blue blankets someone had left with it. As Ben lifted the child, a note fluttered out from the folds of the blanket.

Sweeping a hand down to catch the note, Ben held tight to the baby in his arms. "Let's see what this says."

Carefully Ben balanced the wiggling bundle in his arms, so he could unfold the note and read it over the cries of the baby.

"'Reverend Ben, this is Tyler. He is one month old. I know you will take good care of him.'"

Stunned, Ben dropped the note back into the empty box, then stared blankly down at the little baby boy in his arms.

"Tyler?" The infant answered him with a lusty cry.

"You're probably hungry…and wet," Ben said as he shifted the child in his arms. "And I don't have any food or diapers." Then, in spite of his concern, he smiled. "But I certainly know someone who does."

Sara Conroy glanced up just in time to see the tall man with the baby coming directly toward her. The man, handsome in a gentle kind of way, seemed frantic in his efforts to calm the screaming baby. Sara watched, somewhat amused, as he looked up, his incredible blue eyes latching on to her as he headed down the center of the tidy, colorful classroom. He walked carefully so as to avoid stepping on crawling toddlers in his haste.

"Where's Maggie?" the man asked, his tone breathless in spite of the deep tremor of his voice. "I need her, right now."

Sara raised a hand, then tossed back her shoulder-length curly red hair. "Hold on there, Daddy. What's the problem?" Automatically she reached out to take the baby from him.

"This…" the man said, gladly handing the infant over to her. Scissoring a hand through his curly brown locks, he said, "I found him…in the church…a few minutes ago. He's hungry—" here he wiped one hand down the side of his jeans "—and very wet."

Spurred into action, Sara glanced over the baby in her arms. "You found him?"

Ben let out a long sigh. "Yes. Someone left him on a church pew. I heard him crying—" He stopped, his gaze shifting from the baby to Sara's face. "I'm sorry, I'm Ben Hunter. And you must be Maggie's replacement."

"Sara Conroy." She nodded, then lifted her eyes to meet his. "Calm down, Reverend. He won't break, but we do need to check him over. And we'll have to call social services, of course."

"Why?" Ben watched as she gently settled the bawling baby down on a changing table, then moved her hands expertly over his little, thrashing body.

"Well, this child was obviously abandoned," Sara explained, concern for the baby evident in her words. "We have to alert the proper authorities." She automatically handed him a sanitized baby wipe to clean his hands.

Ben relaxed a little, then leaned into a nearby counter. "You're right, of course. There was a note. His name is Tyler and someone seems to think I can take care of him. Is he…is everything all right?"

"I think so," Sara said. At his doubtful look, she added, "I was a pediatric nurse back in St. Paul. He seems healthy—no fever, no signs of exposure or respiratory problems, but we should have a doctor check him out, just the same."

Ben threw the wipe into a trash can. "I'll call Morgan Talbot. He's the local favorite with all the kids."

Sara nodded. "Yes, I met Dr. Talbot just the other day." Glancing over her shoulder to make sure the other children in her care were safe, she buzzed one of the aides. "Abby, can you bring me a warm bottle of formula from our extra supplies?" Then, while Ben called Dr. Talbot, she changed the baby's soiled diaper and found an extra set of flannel pajamas the day-care center kept on hand in a clothes bin. "We'll get him fed and quiet, at least. He'll probably sleep the morning away, poor little fellow."

After hanging up the phone, Ben watched as Sara Conroy went about her work, amazed at how calm and collected she was. Even with a baby in her arms and children pulling at her long denim skirt, she still managed to somehow keep everything under control. Within minutes, she had Abby entertaining the older children while she sat in a canebacked rocking chair and fed little Tyler.

"You look right at home here," he said a few minutes later as Sara laid the contented Tyler down in a nearby bassinet.

"I love children," she said, her expression growing soft as she gazed down at the baby.

He couldn't help but notice how pretty she looked with her red hair glinting in the bright sunshine that streamed in through the big windows. She had a serene smile, and her eyes were every bit as green as a Minnesota spring, but there was something else about Sara Conroy. She had attitude. Big-city attitude. He could see it in her stance, in the way she carried herself—a little self-assured, a little hard-nosed and tough, maybe a little cynical and wary, and a whole lot weary. Sara Conroy would not take anything off anybody, he imagined.

Even a small-town minister who hadn't quite found his footing and certainly didn't want to part with his heart ever again.

"Well, you don't have to stare," Sara said, causing Ben to quickly glance away and then back, a grin on his face.

"Sorry, it's just…you're not from around these parts. St. Paul, did you say?"

"Yeah, but last time I checked, St. Paul women look and act pretty much the same as other women, especially when a handsome man keeps staring at them."

He actually blushed. "I'm sorry. It's…it's just been one of those mornings. First, finding the baby, then finding…you. Not your typical Monday morning."

She lifted a slanted brow. "You were expecting Maggie, right?"

He nodded. "Yeah. I forgot she's out on extended maternity leave. Doctor's orders. She can't risk losing that baby."

"That's why I'm here," Sara said, motioning for him to come into the little office just off the nursery. Turning as Ben followed her, she settled down in the desk chair and smiled up at him. "Have a seat. Less noise in here. We can talk while Abby reads to the children."

"Is that really why you're here?" he asked, surprising himself and Sara. "I mean, why would you give up being a pediatric nurse to work in a church day-care center?''

Sara took her time in answering. "I guess that's a fair question."

"But none of my business?"

"No, no." She held up a hand. "It's okay, really. It's just hard sometimes."

"Then you don't have to talk about it."

But she needed to talk about it and he seemed like a good listener. Being a minister probably made him an expert listener. And it certainly didn't hurt that he was intriguing in his shy, quiet way, and handsome in a rugged, unpolished way. Completely opposite from Steven.

Not wanting to dwell on her ex-fiancé and his many flaws, Sara shrugged then said, "My mother died recently. She had Alzheimer's and it was up to me to take care of her in her final days. Once it was all over, I realized I needed a break, something less stressful. Maggie suggested I come here, to take her place for a while."

He leaned back on a table. "I'm sorry about your mother. That must have been very hard on you."

"It was," she replied, some of the brightness leaving her eyes. "It wasn't easy, watching her deteriorate right before my eyes. But…we always depended on each other. She didn't have anyone else. It was up to me."

Ben reached out a hand to touch hers. "Sounds like you did need a break. Maggie is good at suggesting things like that. She cares about people."

"She saved my life," Sara said, then instantly regretted it. "I mean—she called me at exactly the right time. I was on my last legs. Just exhausted."

"Physically and spiritually," Ben added, his blue eyes filled with compassion and understanding.

"Yes, I suppose so." Refusing to give in to the luxury of self-pity, Sara stood up. "But I'm doing okay. I'm all settled in out on the lake and I do love the peacefulness of this place. Less hectic than the big city."

Ben lifted off the table to follow her out into the long, colorful nursery. "But not nearly as exciting?"

Sara's little bubble of a laugh magnified her dimples.

"What's so funny?" Ben asked, captivated.

"Well, Reverend, I'd say my first morning here has been rather exciting, don't you think?"

"Yes, I guess it has." He glanced down at Tyler's pink face. "He's a handsome baby, isn't he?"

"Beautiful," Sara said, the word filled with awe. "I wonder why someone would abandon him like that."

"I don't know," Ben replied. "And why with me, of all people?"

Sara gave him another direct look, again taking her time to answer. "Because, like the note said—whoever left Tyler with you thinks you can take care of him. And I think maybe they're right."

"You think that—based on me rushing in here

to hand this baby over to the first person I could find?''

"I think that—based on the concerned expression on your face when you brought him, the way you handled him and the way you looked down at him when we finally got him settled. I've worked with a lot of parents and children, Reverend, and it's taught me to be a pretty good judge of character." She lifted her head, then folded her arms over her leaf-patterned sweater. "Besides, Maggie has already sang your praises. And that's good enough for me."

Her smile was full of confidence and assurance. But Ben didn't feel so confident or so assured. "We'll have to see about all of that," he said, looking up to see Dr. Morgan Talbot weaving his way through the toys and toddlers in the room. "I don't want to disappoint you, or Maggie, but I'm not sure I'm up to taking care of an infant."

Sara grabbed Ben's shirtsleeve. "You're not thinking of sending him away, are you?"

Ben hesitated, then whispered. "I just thought foster parents might be better equipped—"

Sara shook her head. "They left the baby with you. You can't send little Tyler away without even trying to help him."

Morgan came in, smiled at them, then went right to Tyler's bed. "Well, well, Reverend, let's have a look at your little bundle of joy."

Ben glanced at his friend, then back to the red-haired, obviously determined woman flashing green fire at him. "I just don't know—"

"I'll help you," she offered, shocking herself in the process. "I'll help you with Tyler. You should keep him here, surrounded by people who care, until we can decide what to do about him. I'm sure social services will agree."

Ben could only nod. She certainly seemed determined to keep the baby nearby, but he wasn't so sure. He wasn't so sure at all. This was just one more burden, one more test, and he didn't think he could bear up underneath much more.

But Ben knew that God didn't always send His answers in the easiest, most convenient packages. Sometimes they came in the form of crying babies and red-haired women with attitude. Whether you wanted them to or not.

"The baby is in good shape," Morgan told Ben later as they both stood over the bassinet. "He looks completely healthy to me."

"That's a relief, at least," Ben said, one hand automatically touching the tiny fingers of the sleeping infant.

"What are you going to do about him?" Morgan asked, a faint smile on his lips.

"That's a good question." Ben let out a sigh, then glanced around the empty nursery. Sara and Abby had taken the other children outside for some fresh air before lunch and nap time. "I don't think I'm qualified to care for a baby."

"Someone obviously thought you were."

"Well, that someone obviously wasn't thinking this thing through." He shook his head, then turned to stare out the window where the children toddled here and there on the miniature playground equipment. "I've got a meeting with a woman from social services in a few minutes, to decide. Sara seems to think I should keep Tyler here for a little while at least."

"Sara?" Morgan glanced in the direction of his friend's gaze. "Oh, that Sara. She comes highly recommended, you know. A friend of Maggie's, I believe, from college. And fast becoming a friend of Rachel's, too. My wife met Sara after church yesterday when she went over to visit with Maggie."

"She's nice enough," Ben admitted, his eyes on the smiling woman sitting in a pile of leaves, surrounded by children. He had to smile when she let one of the toddlers drop leaves on top of her head. As she shook her long, wavy hair and laughed, the varying shades of red and orange foliage merged with the brilliant auburn of her shining curls. "Maybe she should take Tyler. She was a pediatric nurse, and she seems to love her work here."

"They didn't leave Tyler at her door, friend," the doctor reminded him. "They left the baby with you."

"So you're casting your lot with Sara?"

"I'm casting my lot with you, Reverend. I trust

you to do what is best for this child. And for yourself.''

Ben whirled to stare at his friend. "And what's that supposed to mean?''

"Oh, nothing. Nothing at all." Morgan grabbed his wind jacket and started for the door. "You've just seemed…well, a bit restless lately, Ben. Like you're not quite settled.''

"I don't know that I am settled. Every time I think I've won the congregation over, something comes up and I'm right back in the middle of a dispute.''

"Give them time," Morgan told him with a friendly hand on his arm. "Some of these members have been in this church for well over thirty years. They are definitely set in their ways.''

Ben nodded. "And dead set against me and my newfangled changes. Last week, someone complained because I played the guitar during the service. Said he liked the pipe organ just fine, thank you very much. You'd think after three years—''

"Yeah, you'd think," Morgan said, grinning. "Three years is not much time, considering Reverend Olsen was their minister for most of his life—and thankfully, he never attempted to play any instruments. You've at least got him beat in that particular talent.''

"He was a very patient man," Ben said as he waved Morgan out the door. "I'll be all right. Finding a baby at my door has just thrown me for a loop. Hey, tell Sara I'm going to wait in here for the police and social services.''

"Okay." Morgan gave him a salute, then called, "How about a game of one-on-one this afternoon? I think it's my turn to win."

Ben nodded. "Okay, hoops on the church court, right after work."

"I'll see you then."

Ben turned back to the sleeping baby, taking the time to enjoy the quiet that had fallen over the usually noisy room. He closed his eyes and stood there for just a minute, a silent prayer forming in his heart. *Lord, show me what to do.*

Then he lifted his head, his gaze searching out the intriguing woman who'd already issued him a challenge. Sara glanced up at him, waved, then grabbed a cute little blond-haired girl and lifted her onto the tiny swing. Soon she had the child going back and forth in an arc of rainbow swirls. They sure made a pretty picture.

So pretty, that Ben had to look away. He'd often thought he'd have a family one day, but it wasn't meant to be. He was alone again, with not a sound to disturb him.

Except for the faint, rhythmic breathing of the baby someone had left in his care.

Chapter Two

"We really don't have much choice."

Betty Anderson looked at the crowd of people gathered in her office at The Old First Church Daycare Center, her reading glasses tipped precariously on the end of her pert nose. "I think Ben will make a fine temporary guardian for Tyler."

"I agree." The chief of police, Samuel Riley, a short, round man with white hair and a beard that always got him the part of Santa in the church Christmas functions, nodded his head so vigorously that his ruddy double chin rolled up against his chest. "Ben, with all this red tape we have to wade through with social services and child welfare, and given the fact that we've never had anything like this occur in Fairweather, I think you're the best candidate for taking care of the baby at this point—just until we can weigh all the facts and find out exactly what the proper procedure is around here."

"It would only be for a few days, a week at most," Betty pointed out. "And, Ben, you know we'll all pitch in. You can bring Tyler here every day during the week. Sara has already agreed to watch him for you—whenever you need her to." Her smile indicated she was immensely pleased with Sara's offer.

"I'll even go over the basics with you, step by step," Sara told him, that glint of a challenge in her green eyes.

"I appreciate that," Ben replied, his eyes touching on Sara Conroy's face as he sat back in his chair. It was late in the day and Tyler was safe in the infant room with all the other children. But it had been a long and trying day for Ben. Not only had he had to go round and round with the police, but the child welfare office in Minneapolis hadn't offered up much help, either. The closest available foster family they could come up with was in St. Paul. And everyone agreed that the baby shouldn't be carted off to the big city—not when he had a loving, supportive community of people right here, willing to help take care of him. The authorities had pulled what strings they could, to keep the child here.

But, ultimately, the responsibility rested with Ben. He didn't want to send the baby away any more than the rest of them. And he was fast losing the battle against his own insecurities and doubts. "I'll need lots of help," he said at last. "I don't know a whole lot about babies."

"You can hold your own," Betty told him as she took off her glasses and came around the desk. "I've seen you with the children right here. They love you." At his doubtful look, she added, "You'll be just fine, Ben."

"Okay." Ben scissored his fingers through his hair, then let out a long sigh. "Guess I'm a temporary father."

Betty patted him on the arm. "I'll have Warren load a bassinet and all the other equipment to take to the parsonage. And I've already been to the grocery store—got you plenty of formula and diapers. And I even bought two of the cutest little outfits—nice and warm, with teddy bears and baseballs."

"Thanks, Betty." Ben got up, then looked over at Sara. She sure seemed amused with all of this. "Well, time to pay up, Miss Conroy. Want to come to my house and show me how to mix up formula?"

"Does this count as our first date?" she teased, in a voice meant for Ben's ears only.

"I didn't think you'd be interested in me, except in a strictly temporary guardian capacity," he shot back. "Since you seemed so determined for me to take this foundling."

Lifting her brows in surprise, she retorted, "Maybe I just wanted an excuse to come and visit you, Reverend."

She was rewarded with another blush. Not used to flirting, or being flirted with, Ben did manage a glib reply. "All you had to do was ask."

Sara laughed, then moved past him. "I'll follow you in my car."

"Do you know the way?"

"Julianne pointed your house out to me when we took a walk at lunch," she told him.

"And just so you'll know," Betty interjected, "Emma has already told Sara that you are single and in need of female companionship."

Ben groaned while Sara nodded, that amused look coloring her face. "And she grilled me, so I'll just go ahead and get the awkward questions out of the way. Yes, I'm single, but no, I'm not interested in any type of long-term commitments, and yes, I just want a little peace and quiet, but yes, I'm more than willing to help you with Tyler."

"So much for our first date," Ben said, an uncomfortable grin pinching his face. Somehow though, he felt disappointed that she'd answered all his questions before he'd even had a chance to ask them. Oh, well, that was probably for the best. He had a full plate—no time for starting a heavy personal relationship, and Sara Conroy struck him as a no-nonsense, tough-minded woman. It would be hard to win her over.

"You don't have to look so relieved," Sara said as they made their way up the hall to the nursery.

Ben felt sheepish and knew he was a coward. "I'm sorry. I've just got a lot on my mind."

"And becoming a temporary father hasn't helped?"

He stopped as they reached the room where the

babies up to one year old spent most of their days while their mothers worked. It was a colorful, playful room with a painted mural of Noah's ark centered on one wall, and various other bright Biblical figures painted on every available surface.

The room was quiet now; most of the parents had already come to claim their little ones and the aides were busy cleaning up for the day. Outside, the burnished sunset that proclaimed Minnesota in the fall shined golden and promising.

"I'll take care of Tyler," he said, more to himself than to Sara. "I just wish I could help the person who left him here. Whoever did it, must have been so desperate, so alone. His mother is probably out there somewhere right now, wondering if she did the right thing."

Sara watched the man standing beside her, and felt a tug at her heartstrings that almost took her breath away.

Almost. Hadn't she just five minutes earlier told Ben in no uncertain terms that she wasn't interested in any kind of romantic relationship? Hadn't she pledged to avoid opening up her heart to that kind of pain ever again?

Remember, Sara, she reminded herself, time and circumstance can ruin any relationship.

That's exactly what had happened with Steven. She'd never had the time to give to him, to nurture what they had together, and because of the circumstances—her mother, his work—he'd taken a job in Atlanta, Georgia, far away from the cold winters

of Minnesota and far away from what he'd termed
her cold heart.

But this man, this man would understand why
she'd had to sacrifice so much for her own work
and her mother's illness. This man, this gentle, kind
man, would do the same thing. He was doing the
same thing by taking in Tyler.

Somehow, knowing that warmed her, melting
away the layers of hardness she'd wrapped around
her heart. But with that warmth came a warning—
to take care, to be cautious.

Time and circumstance could once again bring
her pain. She only had a little time here before
she'd have to make a decision regarding her job
back in St. Paul, and she wouldn't let the circumstance of an abandoned baby trick her into thinking
she, too, could find a good life with someone like
Ben Hunter.

Besides, the man was a minister, a preacher, a
man of God. And she was definitely not preacher's
wife material.

As she watched Ben lift baby Tyler out of his
crib and bundle him in a thick cotton blanket, she
regretted that. Ben would make the right woman a
fine husband. Except her. Except Sara Conroy. No,
she was too cynical, too burned-out and disillusioned for someone like Ben Hunter. She wasn't
the right woman, and she had to remember that.

"I think I can remember all of this," Ben said
hours later as he tucked the baby in, hopefully for

a few hours of sleep at least. "Sterilize the bottles every night, mix the formula, put it in the refrigerator, heat it till it feels warm on my skin." He shook an empty bottle toward his wrist to demonstrate. "Feed him every three or four hours, regardless of what time it is, until he gets on a schedule. Change diapers as needed—what?"

Sara couldn't help the laughter bubbling over in her throat. But she couldn't possibly tell Ben that he looked so incredibly adorable, standing there in his flannel shirt and old jeans with a burp cloth slung over his shoulder and his dark curls all mushed up against his forehead, while one of the three cats he owned meowed at his feet. "It's nothing," she said, "You just look so helpless."

"I am not helpless," Ben retorted in mock defiance. "Well, not as long as you're here, at least."

She took another sip of her coffee, ignoring the little tremors of delight his innocent statement brought to her stomach. "Oh, I think you'll be just fine. From all the phone calls you've received, I'd say you've got more than enough help."

"You're right there. My congregation has really surprised me with all their support. I was afraid some of them would frown on this—a single man taking in an infant. I'm pleasantly surprised, and very grateful."

"Maybe you don't give yourself enough credit," she said as he refilled her coffee. "Of course, I've heard a lot about Reverend Olsen—hard shoes to fill."

"He was the best. I still visit him in the nursing home and sometimes I bring him here, just to spend an afternoon with me. He is the wisest man I know and I respect his suggestions, even if I don't always follow them."

"I see," she said, smiling back at him. "You want to do things your way."

"Sometimes, but I find that I mostly have to do things His way." He pointed heavenward.

"An awesome task," Sara retorted, meaning it. She had long ago stopped trying to figure out God's plan for her life. Now she was taking things one day at a time.

"Do you plan to come to church, hear one of my sermons?"

The question, so direct, so sincere, threw her. "I...I probably will." Lowering her head, she added, "I haven't been very regular in my faith lately. In fact, I think I kind of gave up on it."

"Losing a loved one can do that to you," Ben said, his head down, his whole stance seeming to go weary.

His tone was so quiet, so introspective, that Sara wondered if he'd suffered such a loss himself. Not wanting to pry, she stayed silent, helping him put away the many supplies required to feed and care for a baby. "I'm better now. I was bitter for a while—about my mother's illness, about life in general. And I hope coming here will help me to...to find some sense of peace."

He turned to her then, his gentle smile reminding

her that although this man was different, a man of strong faith no doubt, maybe he was still just as vulnerable to pain and frustration as the rest of humankind.

Leaning close, he said, "I hope you find your peace here, Sara. This is certainly a good place to start."

Is that why he'd come here? she wondered. Before she could ask him to tell her, he lifted off the counter and turned away. "Let's sit down and catch our breaths."

Then he dropped the diaper and grabbed his own coffee cup, motioning for Sara to follow him into the tiny sitting room of the cottage he called home. The room, like many of the rooms she'd noticed in the charming, old house, was in a state of repair.

"Sorry about the boards and nails," he told her as he offered her the comfortable old leather armchair near the fireplace. "I fully intend to finish that wall of bookcases, and all the other work around here—someday. But I'm not the handyman type. I'll have to get Warren Sinclair to repair my repairs, I'm afraid."

The small kitten that had been meowing at Ben's feet, aptly named Rat because he was a deep gray and tended to skitter like a mouse, hurriedly followed them into the room, then jumped up on her lap the minute she sat down.

Sara nodded as she glanced around the cozy room. Books everywhere—that didn't surprise her—and a few unpacked boxes coupled with very few personal touches. In spite of the volumes of philosophy and poetry and religious tomes, in spite of the clutter and typical male chaos, it looked as if Ben was just a visitor here—not really settled in yet. Maybe that was why he was afraid of taking on little Tyler. He wasn't ready for any permanent commitments, either.

Since she knew that feeling, she shrugged. "I like it. It has potential."

"Somewhere underneath all the old paint and leaking roof, and all my many messes, yes, there is a lot of potential for this to once again become a showcase."

Sara thought the current occupant had a lot of potential, too, but she didn't voice that opinion. "I'd better get out to the lake," she said instead. "It's getting late and we both have an early day tomorrow."

Ben held up a hand in protest. "I could warm up some of that stew Emma sent over. Or we could just go for the oatmeal cookies."

"Reverend, are you stalling the inevitable?"

Ben lowered his head. "Yeah, I admit it. I'm terrified about being alone with that baby. What if I don't know how to handle his cries?"

"Your cats seem to be thriving—even if they are fur balls instead of humans. You must know something about nurturing babies."

He grinned, then rolled his eyes. "Emma thinks I'm the humane society. But taking care of little

Rat and his fuzzy companions is a tad different from providing for a baby.''

"Just hold him," she said on a soft voice, her eyes meeting his in the muted lamplight. "That's what most babies want and need the most."

"Most humans," he echoed, his voice warm and soothing, his eyes big and blue and vastly deep.

"Yes, I suppose so."

Because the conversation had taken an intimate twist, and because for some strange reason she herself felt an overwhelming need to be held, Sara placed the still-whining Rat on the braided rug at her feet and got up to leave. "You can call me, day or night."

"Even at 3:00 a.m.?"

Imagining his sleep-filled voice at three o'clock in the morning didn't help the erratic charges of awareness coursing through her body. "Anytime," she managed to say. Why did his eyes have to look so very blue?

"I'll hold you to that," he told her as he escorted her to the front door. "Drive carefully."

"I will. It's only a few miles."

"I'll see you tomorrow then."

"Tomorrow." She hurried out to her car, not daring to take a breath until she was sure he couldn't see her. What on earth had come over her, anyway? Her first day in a new town, her first day on the job, and the first eligible man to walk through the door already had her nerves in a shamble and her heart doing strange pitter-pattering things that it shouldn't be doing at all.

It's just the stress, she decided. She'd been through so much—first Steven's decision to transfer to Atlanta—with or without her, then her mother's inevitable death, then the hospital telling her she might want to consider an extended leave of absence because she was exhausted and not too swift on her feet. It had all been just too much for one person.

Maggie's call had come at exactly the right time, but now Sara had to wonder if she'd made the right decision, coming here. She only wanted to concentrate on the children in her care, enjoy the less stressful, much slower way of life here, go home each night to her quiet cottage, and stare out at the endless blue waters of Baylor Lake.

That's all she needed right now—time to decide where she wanted to go in her life, time to heal from the grief of watching her mother deteriorate right before her eyes, time to accept that Steven wasn't coming back for her and that she wouldn't get that family she'd always dreamed about.

If she let herself get involved with the town preacher, she wouldn't know any peace, none at all. But she could be a friend to Ben Hunter, and she could help him with little Tyler. That at least would ease some of her loneliness.

And his, too, maybe.

Ben's kindness, his gentle sense of nobility, had touched on all her keyed-up, long-denied emotions.

That was why she felt this way—all shook up and disoriented. Throw in an adorable, abandoned baby, and well, any woman would start getting strange yearnings for home and hearth, strange maternal longings that would probably never be fulfilled. Any woman would feel completely and utterly lonely, sitting in her car in the cold.

"I'll be all right," she told herself as she drove toward the charming cottage she'd rented at Baylor Lake. "I'll be all right. I came here to find some time, to heal, to rethink my life. Not to get attached to a poetic preacher and a sweet lost little baby."

But somehow she knew in her heart that she had already formed a close bond with those two, a bond that would be hard to forget, even given time and circumstance.

Chapter Three

In a blur of baby, blankets and bags, Ben Hunter stepped inside the outer reception room to his church office, thankful that the cold morning air didn't have a hint of snow. That would come soon enough in November. And he couldn't imagine having to dress a wiggling, tiny baby in a snowsuit. It had taken him twenty extra minutes just to get Tyler in the fleece button-up outfit Betty had thoughtfully supplied.

"Oh, there you are."

Emma Fulton got up to come around her desk, her blue eyes flashing brightly as she cooed right toward Tyler. "Let me see that precious child, Reverend Ben."

Ben didn't hesitate to turn the baby over to Emma. The woman had five grandchildren, so she knew what to do with a baby.

"He had a good night," Ben said, letting out a breath as he dropped all the paraphernalia he'd brought along onto a nearby chair. "He was up around four, but other than that, we did okay."

"Of course you did," Emma said, still cooing and talking baby talk. "Even if the good reverend does look a little tired." Pointing her silvery bun toward the small kitchen just off her office, she said, "There's pumpkin bread."

"Bless you," Ben replied, heading straight to the coffeepot. "Somehow I didn't manage to get breakfast." With a grin he called over his shoulder, "But Tyler sure had his. That little fellow can go through a bottle."

"He's a growing boy," Emma replied as she danced a jig with the baby. "Oh, my, look at that. He's laughing. He likes his aunt Emma."

"Well, go ahead," Ben teased as he came back into the room with a chunk of the golden-brown bread, "tell him you were Strawberry Festival Queen in...what year was that, Emma?"

"Never you mind what year, kid. Just remember who you're dealing with here." Her smile belied her defensive tone.

"I always remember who's the boss around here," Ben admonished. Then when he heard someone clearing his throat in his office, he turned to Emma. "Visitor?"

"Oh, I almost forgot." She whirled with the baby in her arms. "Finish your breakfast first. It's Mr. Erickson."

Ben immediately put down his coffee and the last of his bread. "Maybe he's heard something from Jason."

"Don't know," Emma whispered, her expression turning sad. "Want me to take Tyler to the nursery for you?"

"Would you mind?" Ben gathered the baby's things for her. "Tell Sara I'll be over in a little while to check on him and give her a report about his first night with me."

"I certainly will do that," Emma said, getting her smile back in a quick breath, her eyes perfectly centered on the baby.

Ben knew that look. Emma would try to match him up with Sara. Somehow, the thought of that didn't bother him nearly as much as it should—considering Emma had tried to match him up with every single woman in Fairweather, usually with disastrous results. With Sara Conroy, he couldn't foresee any disaster, other than the one in which he might lose his heart. And he wasn't willing to risk that just yet.

As he entered the quiet confines of his office, however, another type of disaster entered his mind. Richard Erickson stood looking out over the prayer garden, his hands tucked in the pockets of his dark tailored wool suit pants, his graying hair trimmed into a rigid style, just the way he ran the local bank and most of this town.

Ben dreaded another confrontation with the man, but his heart had to go out to Mr. Erickson. His only son, sixteen-year-old Jason, had run away from home several months ago.

"Hello, Mr. Erickson," Ben said, extending his hand as the older man pivoted to stare at him with a look of condemnation mixed with a condescending air.

The handshake was quick and unmeaningful, but Richard Erickson was too polite and straitlaced to behave without the impeccable manners that befit a descendant of the founding family of the town. Ben gave him credit for that much, at least.

"Reverend."

"What can I do for you this morning? Any word from Jason, sir?"

At the mention of his youngest child's name, Richard Erickson's whole demeanor changed. After having three daughters, his son, Jason, had been his pride and joy, and ultimately, the child of which he made the most demands and held the highest expectations.

His expression became etched with regret and pride. "No. I was hoping you might have heard something. He did call you before."

"You know I would call you immediately if Jason tried to contact me," Ben told him. "I'm sorry, but I haven't heard anything since the last call back in September."

"Are you sure you'd tell me if you did?"

Ben could see the hostility in the man's brown eyes. It still galled him that this man who contributed so much financially to the church, could not contribute anything emotionally to Ben or his ministry, or to his son Jason, for that matter. Yet Ben didn't have the heart to tell Richard Erickson that part of the reason his son was missing today was because of Mr. Erickson's cold, distant relationship with the boy.

Jason had confided in Ben, and he wouldn't break that confidence. Early on, right after Jason had left, Ben had tried to sit down with Richard and Mary Erickson and explain what Ben had told him. He'd gotten to know the boy pretty well, after serving as coach for the church basketball team.

But the Ericksons would not listen to Ben's concerns. They had told him in no uncertain terms that they blamed him for interfering in their relationship with their son, that Ben's influence had put new-fangled notions in the boy's head and caused him to rebel.

Now, however, Ben was their only source of comfort, since Jason had contacted him on two different occasions after running away earlier in the year. For that reason, and for Jason's sake, Ben swallowed his own resentment and tried to counsel the couple—when they would let him.

Sensing that Richard needed to talk, Ben gestured to a floral armchair. "Please, sit down."

"I don't have much time," Richard said, but he did sit on the very edge of the chair, his back straight, his expression grim. "I just wanted to tell you—if you hear from my son again, you have to let me know. My wife is beside herself—what with the holidays coming up and everything. And all our efforts to track him down have only brought us disappointment.''

"I understand, sir,'' Ben said, his hands folded over his heavily marked desk pad calendar. "I will do whatever I can to convince Jason to come home. I hope you realize that.''

"I realize,'' Richard Erickson said as he rose to leave, "that my son is deeply troubled and that I hold you partially responsible for whatever brought him to this extreme.'' He held up a hand then. "But I do appreciate your efforts on Jason's behalf, and in light of this new situation, I just wanted to remind you where your priorities should be.''

"I'm afraid I don't quite understand,'' Ben said, getting up to follow Erickson out of the office. "What are you trying to tell me, Mr. Erickson?''

Richard Erickson stopped at the door, then turned to face Ben, the look in his eyes devoid of any compassion or understanding. "Taking in a stray baby, an orphan? Come on, Reverend, we both know that you have no business trying to take care of an infant. You should be concentrating on taking care of your congregation, I still get complaints about you, you know. And this latest development hasn't helped matters, not one bit.''

Shocked and angry beyond words, Ben gripped the edge of Emma's desk in order to regain his composure. "You don't need to worry about Tyler, Mr. Erickson. I know what I'm doing and I don't intend to let taking care of this baby interfere with my work here. Rest assured, I know what my responsibilities are."

"Do you?" Erickson pointed a finger in the air. "If you had concentrated on preaching instead of sports, my son might be here today. But you had to form that basketball team, just to glorify yourself. You had to prove that you were the best in college, so you got these local boys all worked up about basketball and winning. Jason didn't have any complaints in life until you came along. Then all he could think about was practice. He was neglecting his studies, getting behind in school. He changed right before our eyes. And now you're planning on raising a baby?"

Ben couldn't believe the things coming out of Richard Erickson's mouth. The man had a skewered idea of what had brought his son to such desperate measures.

Hoping to set him straight, Ben said, "Jason had problems long before I came into the picture, sir. If you'd only listen—"

"I'm done listening to you, Reverend. And I have a good mind to call the authorities and tell them what I know about you. You are not fit to raise that baby, and by trying to prove yourself once again, you will fail. And this church will suffer even more for it. Maybe you should have thought about that, before you took on this new challenge."

Ben looked up to see Sara Conroy standing in the hallway that led to the small narthex of the church. She must have come in from the other side, and from the frozen expression on her face, she'd obviously heard most of their conversation.

Feeling defeated, but refusing to give in to Richard Erickson's rigid attitude, Ben sighed, then asked God for guidance. The very thought of this man trying to have Tyler taken from him only reinforced Ben's close bond with the baby. "I can take care of that baby. I have plenty of people more than willing to help me through this"

"I can change all of that easily enough," Erickson stated, the threatening tone in his words leaving no doubt that he would do just that.

"But you won't," Ben said, his own stance just as rigid. "You wouldn't do that to an innocent child, would you?" When the man didn't answer, he added, "Sir, you can do what you want to me, you can blame me for Jason's problems, too, if that makes you feel better. But don't do anything to jeopardize Tyler. He's very young and very alone right now, and if you interfere, he'll just be snatched away again. Do you really want that on your conscience?"

His words seemed to calm the older man. Richard Erickson looked up then and realized they weren't alone anymore. The manners set in immediately. As he lifted a hand to Sara in greeting, his whole expression softened.

"I've got too much to deal with as it is," he said at last, his voice low now. "But I'm warning you,

you'd better watch your step. And you'd better hope I find my son soon.''

"I'll pray for that day and night, just as I've been doing,'' Ben told him, meaning it. ''If you need anything—''

"I don't.'' With that, Erickson nodded to Sara, then turned and headed out the door to his luxury sedan.

Sara took one look at Ben and headed straight to him. ''You should sit down.''

He didn't argue with her. Instead, he fell down into Emma's softly padded desk chair, sighed long and hard, then ran a hand through his hair with a groan of frustration. ''Sorry you had to witness that.''

Hoping to lighten the somber mood, Sara said, ''Do you always win over your members in such a sure way?''

"Every last one of them,'' he told her, some of the tension leaving his face. Then he looked up at her. ''Mr. Erickson doesn't like me very much right now. His youngest child, and only son, Jason, ran away from home earlier this year, and he blames me for it.''

"You?'' Shocked, Sara leaned against the corner of the desk, near him, her long khaki skirt rustling as she crossed her legs. ''I thought your job was to save souls, not alienate them.''

"Yeah, me, too, but it doesn't always go that way.''

"Want to talk about it?''

He looked up at her again, taking in those glorious red curls and her mysterious green eyes. She had a few freckles scattered across her pert nose, but the rest of her skin was porcelain white and looked creamy soft. She wore a short, green-and-brown striped heavy cotton sweater that only brought out the red of her hair and the green of her eyes. And brought out the warmth in his heart.

"That's supposed to be my line," he told her by way of an answer.

"Which means you probably don't ever have a chance to vent your own frustrations, right?"

"I have plenty of chances," he replied, his hands resting on the arms of the chair as he leaned back to admire her. "I can talk to God anytime."

"Yeah, right."

"Did you just snort? Are you scoffing at me?"

"I'm not snorting or scoffing at all," she said, then smiled. "Okay, maybe I'm a little cynical right now. I know, I know—God is always there. But you look like you could use a real friend right now, a human friend."

"And you're offering to be that friend?"

"Yes, I guess I am." She pushed away from the desk, leaving a trail of flower-and-spice perfume in her wake. "You know, Emma told me that you wanted me to join you for a slice of her famous pumpkin bread—insisted I come right on over here." She headed into the kitchenette. "But I can't leave the babies with an aide for long. Now, do you want to talk to me about this or not. Time is precious.''

Ben shook his head, laughing as he managed to finally get up out of the chair. ''It will take a long time to explain what you just heard and saw.''

''Well, sorry. Gotta go.'' She had her slice of bread and was already headed out the side door. ''I guess you'll just have to bring Tyler out to the lake, for dinner at my place tonight. Say around six-thirty?''

Ben almost fell back into the chair again. This woman was different, that was for sure. And full of intriguing surprises. ''Miss Conroy, are you asking me for a date?''

''No, Reverend Hunter, I'm just telling you I'll fix you dinner.''

He tipped his head to one side, his smile changing into a grin. ''That Emma—look what she's done now.''

''Oh, you didn't really invite me for breakfast?''

''No, but I'm glad you came by.''

''So, does that mean you'll come for dinner?''

''I didn't know nurses could cook.''

''We're pretty handy with a microwave and a few written instructions,'' she said, giving him an impish smile.

''I'll be there,'' he told her as he walked her down the short hallway.

''With Tyler?''

''With Tyler,'' he said, then added, ''if Richard

Erickson doesn't have him taken away before sundown.''

She heard the humor in his voice, but saw the concern in his eyes, too. "He wouldn't do that, would he?''

"He would and he could. The man is very bitter right now and he'd do just about anything to have me removed from this church.''

"We'll just have to say a prayer that he doesn't follow through on his threats, right?''

Ben grabbed at his chest, an expression of mock surprise on his face. "You—you're going to pray for me?''

"Hey, I still talk to God on occasion, even if I don't think He's really listening.''

Ben touched her arm then. "He always listens, Sara. You have to know that. After all, He sent you to rescue me this morning, didn't He?''

"That was Emma's doing,'' she said, acutely aware of the clean, fresh smell of baby lotion mixed with aftershave that lifted out around him. "And remind me to thank her later.''

"Are you sure it was all Emma's doing?'' he countered, holding the door for her, but not letting her pass just yet.

"No, I'm not sure of anything right now, except that I need to get back to work. I'll see you tonight, Rev.''

Ben watched her walk across the yard toward the day-care center, her straight skirt swishing, her long booted legs carrying her on her merry way. He didn't know if God had sent Sara to him, but she had come just in time, he decided.

Because she was right. He could use a friend. He was blessed with several well-meaning friends here in the church and he appreciated how Emma and Betty stood by him and fought for him, but he needed someone to share quiet moments with, someone he could really open up to and talk with. And Sara Conroy fit the bill—almost too perfectly.

Yet, she'd set the ground rules, and as long as they stuck by them, they'd both be okay. She was willing to be his friend, and she was willing to help with Tyler. Surely there could be no harm in that.

Ben decided he did need her help—he needed Sara to show him how to be a good surrogate dad to Tyler. And he wouldn't lose Tyler. Richard Erickson's threats had made Ben even more determined to keep the baby safe and near. Somehow he had to show Jason's bitter father that he was fit to take care of the little baby, and fit to take care of this congregation, too.

And somehow he hoped God would hear all of their prayers and show Jason Erickson the way back home again.

Chapter Four

"So, because you stepped in and tried to counsel this boy, his father now blames you for his running away?"

Sara held her fork on her plate, her gaze falling across Ben's troubled face. He'd just told her, between bites of salad and spaghetti, about Jason Erickson and his prominent, immensely wealthy family.

"That about sums things up," Ben replied as he snagged another crusty piece of French bread then dipped it into the sauce on his plate. "And maybe Mr. Erickson is right."

"I see," Sara replied, laying her fork down to stare over at him. "So now you're beginning to blame yourself, too? Ben, from everything you just told me, it sounds as if you did all you could to help this boy. It's not your fault he felt forced to run away from home."

Ben dropped his bread on his plate, then sat back in his chair with a long sigh. "But did I cause this? I've asked myself that same question over and over in the last few months. I encouraged the boy to come out of his self-protective shell, to open up to me, and I also encouraged him to get involved with the church basketball team—something his father apparently didn't approve of at all."

"But you have to remember that by doing those things you opened up a whole new world to Jason. It sounds as if he needed an outlet—precisely to keep him out of trouble and give him some confidence, and you gave him that outlet."

Ben gave a little nod of agreement and straightened up in his chair. "He loved the game and he had a natural talent for it. But he'd been struggling in school and I'm afraid all the practices and the heavy schedule did make matters worse. I tutored him, but—"

"But—nothing," Sara said, getting up to refill their water glasses. As she walked by the coffeepot, she flipped the On button and started a fresh brew for later. "Something else must have triggered his leaving. I can't believe a few bad grades would make him do something so desperate."

Ben leaned back in his chair again, and Sara watched as he surveyed the quaint little kitchen decorated with various antique cooking utensils and dozens of potted plants which she hoped she could keep alive through the winter.

"His grades had actually improved a little. And

he was trying so hard to please his father and still maintain his own identity. I just wish I knew what really happened.''

''When was the last time you saw him?''

''In April of this year. He came by the office to do some homework, but his mind wasn't on it. He seemed distracted, worried. I tried to find out what was wrong, but he wouldn't talk and I just thought he was nervous about the history test he had the next day.'' Rubbing a hand across his chin, he added, ''But I've talked to him on the phone a couple of times since then. He won't contact his parents, so I've tried to encourage him to let me help him, but he refuses to tell me what's going on. I should have tried to help him, make him tell me what was wrong, way back when I had the chance.''

''You had no way of knowing,'' Sara said as she set a plate of cookies on the table, then indicated to Ben to take one. ''Emma sends her love along with her special tea cakes.''

That perked Ben up. ''I've had her tea cakes,'' he said as he snared one and bit into it. ''Mmm, good.''

''Let's take these delicious cookies and our coffee into the den,'' Sara told him, hoping to take his mind off Jason. ''That way we can check on little Tyler, too.''

Ben followed her, carrying the plate of cookies. ''He's sleeping away. I think he likes the fire.''

Sara smiled down at the baby. They'd fixed him

up a blanketed bed on a deep arm chair near the fire, safe with pillows all around. "He does look content. You apparently did a good job on your first day as his guardian."

"I was a nervous wreck," Ben admitted as he settled down on the matching floral couch, then glanced over at the sleeping baby.

As she sat down in another armchair, Sara had to admit it felt good, having them both here in her new home. It didn't seem nearly as lonely tonight.

The room was long and narrow, with a dozen or so paned windows that allowed a sweeping view of the lake down below the tree-shaded hills. In the summer, the windows could be thrown open to the fresh country air, but tonight Sara had them shut tight against the approaching chill of winter.

Ben looked at Tyler, his expression thoughtful and hopeful. "I think that's why I'm determined to help this child—after all of this with Jason, I mean. I let Jason slip away, but maybe this...maybe this is another chance for me, having Tyler to look after."

Sara's heart went into another telltale spin. Oh, she didn't want to feel these things she was beginning to feel. But Ben Hunter looked so sweet, so scared, so lost, sitting there with the firelight reflecting in his blue eyes. Funny, how she'd always assumed ministers just had pat answers for every situation, that they coped above and beyond anything ordinary humans had to endure. But being around Ben Hunter had taught her that even a man of God was still a human being, with feelings and emotions just like anyone else.

Yet, this particular minister did his very best to shield the rest of the world from his own innermost thoughts and torments. Which was why she was worried about him now.

She could tell by the way he talked about the baby, that he was already forming a strong bond with little Tyler. What would happen when the authorities made a decision regarding the baby? What if Ben became too attached to the little boy?

"Ben, you realize you might not have Tyler for very long, don't you?"

"Oh, sure," he said, but it sounded hollow in the silent room. "Don't give me that doubtful look. I know I won't be able to keep him. But at least while he's here, I can give him all the love and nurturing that I've got."

"And you've sure got a lot, from what I can tell."

He looked up at her then, his cookie in midair, his expression warm, his eyes questioning. "How do you know that? We've only known each other a couple of days now."

Sara shifted in her chair, wishing she'd learn not to blurt out whatever popped into her head. "Well, you seem to have a good rapport with your congregation, Mr. Erickson aside. And I feel as if I knew you already, before I even met you, thanks to Maggie's accurate description."

Yes, Maggie had told her Ben was handsome and

sensitive, a good minister. Maybe that was why Sara seemed so attracted to him—she'd come into this with already-high expectations. She shrugged, uncomfortable with the whole conversation. "Emma thinks you hung the moon, and Betty is always singing your praises."

There. That explained it. Everyone thought Ben was perfect, so naturally, Sara would just *assume* that he was. She'd been brainwashed, obviously. Surely there was a flaw hiding behind that captivating grin and those incredible blue eyes.

His gaze didn't waver. "They have both been a tremendous help to me, that's for sure."

Because he was staring at her with that bemused, confused expression plastered across his face, because the room was growing exceptionally warm, Sara hopped up. "Want some more coffee or more cookies?"

"No, I want to know why you think I'm such a lovable guy?"

Flustered, she sank back down on the overstuffed chair. "Well, because...you're a preacher. Isn't lovable a prerequisite?"

"I suppose, but I've known some cold, unlovable ministers in my time."

Seizing on that, she threw out a hand. "There, you see! You obviously aren't one of those. You know how to connect with people, draw people out. I'm surprised you're still single."

Her soft, mortified moan only made Ben laugh. "You like me, don't you?"

Sara hung her head, hoping her mop of curls would hide the red in her face. "Of course, I *like* you. You've been a good friend, and you've made me feel very welcome here. And since we've agreed to share the responsibility of taking care of Tyler—"

"That would naturally make us have to stay in close contact, right?"

"Right—so that's why I'm just...glad that you're—"

"Such a lovable guy?"

"Yes, exactly." She slapped her palm on her lap, her gaze centered on the fire. "It would be hard to maintain a relationship—I mean, a friendship—with someone who was distant and uncaring."

The bemused expression shifted into something more confident and self-assured. "So, we've agreed that we'll share in Tyler's well-being, and we've agreed that we have some sort of relationship—I mean, friendship—developing here."

She squirmed, straightened a stack of magazines on the table, then crossed one booted leg over the other one. "Yes, I think we can safely agree on those two things."

Ben took a bite of his cookie. "Well, I'm glad we got that settled."

Sara looked up at him at last, and seeing the amusement in his eyes, ventured a nervous smile herself. "I feel like a complete idiot."

"Why? Because you had to admit you like me? I'm flattered, of course, but I promise I won't fall at your feet with undying gratitude and embarrass you any further.''

''Thanks for that, at least.'' She got up to stir the fire, which was blazing right along with no intent of going out—just like the one burning in her belly. ''Ben, I was engaged—''

He sat up, another cookie uneaten in his hand. ''Are you about to tell me you're not ready for anything long-term and heavy?'' In spite of the lighthearted nature of his words, Sara sensed the seriousness in his eyes.

''Yes, that's exactly what I'm about to tell you. Steven and I were a couple for years, but...for some reason, we never did really make a strong commitment to each other. We tried, but there was *my* work, and *his* work, and then when my mother got ill—''

''He didn't know how to handle it?''

When his tone became just as serious as his gaze, she turned to face him. ''No, he didn't appreciate my long hours at the hospital, and my refusal to put my mother in a home.''

''What happened?''

''He took a job in Atlanta, Georgia, and he gave me an ultimatum. Either come with him, or the wedding was off.''

''So I guess I know the answer.''

''Yep. Same old story, different chapter.''

''You did what you had to do.''

''That's a rather tired cliché, don't you think?''

''But an accurate one.''

"I couldn't leave my mother."

At the anguish in her voice, Ben dropped the forgotten cookie back on the plate and came to stand by her in front of the fire. "No, you couldn't do that, and you don't have to explain that to anybody."

He wasn't exactly sure when his hand had moved up to her shoulder, but suddenly he was holding her, hugging her the way he'd hugged hundreds of suffering church members in a time of crisis. "I'm sorry, about your engagement, about your mother. But I'm not sorry you got rid of ol' Steven."

"Oh, really?" Because he held her face crushed against his sweatshirt, it came out muffled.

"Really. Because now you have a chance to get to know a lovable, *nurturing* preacher who needs a lot of help with a little baby boy."

"And his ego, too, apparently," she said as she raised her head, her expression dubious.

Ben looked down at her and felt his heart swelling with a certain need, a need that he hadn't felt or wanted to feel for a very long time. When had this solicitous hug turned into something more intimate, something more...rewarding?

"My ego *is* fragile," he said as his gaze touched on her shining, clouded eyes. Too fragile to tell her his own dark fears and secret regrets.

"Then you know none of this can last, right?"

"You mean, Tyler's being here, you and I being here, together like this?"

"Yes."

The one word held all the defeat he felt in his soul. Yes, he knew this couldn't last, and he didn't really want it to last, did he? This was too close to being perfect; too close to being exactly as he'd envisioned his life so long ago. But he'd envisioned this dream with another woman, and she was gone now. He couldn't bring himself to tell Sara about Nancy just yet. Because he wasn't accustomed to baring his soul to anyone other than God, the pain of losing his own fiancée three years ago was his to bear alone.

"Yes," he echoed, his gaze searching her face, "I know this is all very temporary. I'm not holding my breath, waiting for any sort of commitments, just dealing with what the good Lord has thrown my way."

"You sound so resigned."

He backed away then, sweeping a hand through his hair. "Yes, I guess I am resigned. I've learned the hard way that sometimes the very things you think you want and need, the things you think you can't live without…well, sometimes those very things can be taken from you in a heartbeat."

He glanced over at Sara. The expectant look on her face scared him, forcing him to put a different spin on his own self-pity. "I've seen it so many times—losing someone you love is never easy and there are no easy answers. We tend to lash out at God, because we expect Him to give us answers. But, in the end, we have to wait and pray and hope we find our own peace of mind."

"That's so true. It was like that when I lost my mother and Steven, too. I felt so alone."

Relieved that she seemed satisfied with his pitiful ramblings and gentle platitudes, Ben turned back to her then, his words full of compassion and the trace of bitterness he couldn't hide. "Maybe we should just enjoy our time together and let it go at that."

"Maybe," she replied, the one word full of questions.

Ben didn't miss the disappointment in that one word. He felt that same disappointment in his heart.

But disappointment was so much easier to deal with than real pain.

Ben entered the Book-Stop, a combination bookstore and café located directly on the green in beautiful downtown Fairweather. Intent on finding a book on infant care, he smiled and waved at Frank Wren, the owner, and Maggie's anxious husband.

"How's Maggie?" Ben asked as he made his way to the long wooden counter where Frank was taking inventory of some paperbacks.

"Any day now, Reverend," Frank said in his fast-clipped Minnesota accent. "My wife is ready to have this baby."

"We're all praying for you," Ben told the nervous father-to-be.

But who could blame Frank for being nervous? After trying for five years to have a child, Maggie and Frank had just about given up, and then there had been complications throughout the pregnancy. This child was truly a blessing.

Frank nodded, then replied, "And I'll do the same for you. How's your little one?"

Touched that Frank had referred to Tyler as his own, Ben grinned. "He's amazing. I've only had him a week, but I think he's grown a few inches already. And that's why I'm here, Frank. I need a book on babies."

Frank chuckled, then pointed to a row toward the back of the store. "Got lots of those, but, Rev, they don't make an accurate instruction manual for children. That's what Maggie is always telling me, anyway."

"She would know," Ben said, shaking his head. "She's certainly helped take care of most of the children in Fairweather. And now, her own. She'll be a good mother."

"That I know." Frank pointed back to the shelf. "C'mon, let's see what we can find."

Ben followed Frank's stocky, fast-walking figure to the back of the store. It was late afternoon and he had to get back in time to pick up Tyler from the church nursery. And see Sara, of course.

Like it or not, he was growing closer to Sara Conroy each and every day. Maybe because she was helping him take care of Tyler, and because they worked in the same building, they just naturally ran into each other. Maybe because he liked her, a lot. Maybe because she was pretty and charming and a straight-talker with no secrets to guard.

Well, maybe a few.

Sara was a complete mystery, a mystery that Ben found himself wanting to explore more and more. So he also found himself coming up with little excuses to visit the nursery.

Well, he had to check on Tyler, didn't he? The little baby had become a big part of his life. And he looked forward to taking Tyler home each night, to cuddling with him in the big leather chair by the fire, to telling him stories of the Bible and God's amazing work. A baby, Ben had found out, was easy to talk to, to share secrets with, to open up your heart to. And so was Sara Conroy.

What would he do when they were both gone from his life?

"How 'bout this one?"

Ben looked up to find Frank staring at him, a fat book in his hand.

"That one looks good," Ben said, not even bothering to read the title. Didn't he know Maggie was right? There were no concrete answers to raising a child.

"Of course, you have the best book of all already," Frank told him as they headed back up to the front of the shop.

Still distracted by thoughts of Sara, Ben said, "I do?"

"You do. The Bible, Reverend. All you need to teach a child is right there." Frank pointed to his own worn Bible, lying on a big desk behind the counter.

Ben patted his friend on the arm. "You're right, Frank. And thanks for reminding me."

Frank rang up Ben's purchase. "Want a cup of coffee, some biscotti?"

"No, I have to go pick up Tyler."

Frank grinned. "Well, tell her I said hello."

Confused, Ben lifted a brow. "Excuse me?"

"Sara." Frank winked. "Tell her I said hello. Maggie's wanting to have the two of you over to dinner, but Doc Talbot told her to stay off her feet."

Groaning silently, Ben could only smile. "That's nice of Maggie, but Sara and I...we aren't—"

"A couple?" Frank looked downright disappointed. "That's not what I've been hearing."

"Emma?"

Frank didn't have to acknowledge his sources. Ben knew how much his well-meaning secretary had riding on this match. And it didn't help that Betty Anderson backed her up all the way, and that they both watched a tad too intensely every time Sara and Ben were in a room together.

Not to mention Rachel and Morgan, Julianne and Luke, Warren Sinclair and lately, even Reverend Olsen—the whole town was way too involved in Ben's social life.

Thank goodness the annual Fairweather Harvest Celebration was coming up in a few weeks—planning for that should keep them occupied. They all needed a distraction, to take the heat off *his* back.

Just as Ben started to leave, the phone rang, giving him that much-needed distraction so he wouldn't have to answer any more of Frank's pointed questions. While Frank spoke into the receiver, Ben glanced through the book he'd just purchased, then waved goodbye.

"Rev?" Frank dropped the receiver to come spinning around the counter on one foot. "It's Maggie. It's…the baby." His eyes widened, his next words coming out in a breathless amazement. "The baby is coming."

Ben went into action, since Frank looked helpless. "Come on. I'll drive you. Where to? Is she at the hospital?"

"No, she's at home. We'd better hurry."

"Okay. I'll call Sara from the car and tell her to meet me at the hospital with Tyler. We'll get Maggie to the hospital."

Frank looked doubtful. "I'm scared, Rev."

"Hey," Ben told him as he ushered the excited man out the door, "remember the advice you gave me."

"The Bible," Frank said, a calming sigh moving over his flushed features.

"That's right." Ben gave instructions to another clerk to close up the store, then hurried Frank to his car. "God will take care of everything, my friend."

"That's good," Frank admitted as he slid into

the seat. "Since I seemed to have lost my ability to function properly."

"Don't worry. You're going to be a good father." Ben beamed at his friend, then cranked the car and zoomed toward Frank and Maggie's house. "A father. What a wonderful feeling that must be."

And then it occurred to Ben, he could be a good father, too. To little Tyler. Maybe he could go ahead and adopt the child. That way, he'd never have to suffer the pain of losing him.

Chapter Five

Emma and Sara met them at the hospital.

Emma immediately took charge of the one gurgling baby and all the anxious, joyful adults, sending Maggie and Frank off with the nurses, then turning to Sara and Ben. "You both need to be here for Maggie and Frank, so I'm taking little Tyler home with me. Sam and I will take good care of him."

Touched, but determined to keep Tyler near, Ben shook his head. "Emma, I can't let you do that. You've worked hard all day already."

"Excuse me," Emma replied, a hand on her hip. "I happen to love babies, and Sam has been asking to see Tyler. Besides, you can't keep him here."

"She's right," Sara told him as she smiled down at the wide-eyed baby. "He'd be better off safe and warm at Emma's house, than sitting here in his car seat in this drafty waiting room."

Ben ran a hand through his hair and let out a sigh. He'd never realized just what a tremendous responsibility taking care of an infant could be. "Okay. Emma, I appreciate it. I'll pick him up later."

"Take your time," Emma said, beaming as she began wrapping the baby back in his jacket and blankets.

"There's formula for two bottles in his bag," Sara told her. "But I had just finishing feeding him right before Ben called."

Emma lifted the car seat in her arms, then smiled reassuredly at Ben. "He'll be fine, I promise."

"Spoiled, is more like it," Ben said. With a lop-sided smile, he watched as Emma hefted the baby back out the same doors they'd all just entered minutes before.

With Tyler in good hands, he turned back to standing vigil over Maggie. The nurses had rushed her away the minute Frank escorted her into the emergency room, but the couple had been out of breath and deliriously happy that their baby was finally going to arrive. Now came the waiting part.

Ben was glad to be here, to share in their joy, to offer up prayers of hope and acceptance, whatever the outcome. But he knew in his heart the outcome would be good. Maggie and Frank deserved this bit of happiness.

He looked over at Sara and wondered if he'd ever have the opportunity to rush his wife to the emergency room to give birth to a child. Would he ever even have a wife? Maybe that wasn't in God's plan for his life, but right now he did have little Tyler. And an opportunity to possibly adopt the baby. What would Sara think about this idea?

"Can I get you anything?" Sara asked now, bringing his attention back to the clinical buzz of the tiny, efficient county hospital that served several of the small towns around Fairweather.

"No, I'm fine. Just jittery, I guess. I'm used to christening babies, but this is the first time I've been so involved with a pregnancy and birth."

"I wondered—the way you were staring at me— you looked so serious, I thought maybe you needed to talk or something."

Ben shifted on his feet, looked out at the chilly wintry dusk. He wasn't quite ready to share his latest revelation about possibly adopting Tyler. He had to be sure he was making the right decision. And it was such a big decision. It would change his life forever. So instead of sharing his doubts and dreams with Sara, he focused on the event at hand. "No, I was just thinking how lucky Maggie and Frank are."

"Very." Sara came to stand by him, her gaze following his as he continued to watch the coming nightfall. "Are you thinking about Jason, out there all alone?"

He shrugged, then turned away from the window. "No, actually, I wasn't. Mostly I was being selfish." Then he looked over at her and indicated his head toward the double doors leading to the emergency room. "I want what they have."

Sara was so caught off guard, she had to grip the windowsill to keep from showing her surprise. How was it possible that at the very moment she'd been standing here, watching Ben and thinking how wonderful it would be to have a family of her own, he'd been looking at her and thinking the same thing?

She had to do something, say something, but he just kept standing there, watching her with those poetic, almost sad, all-knowing eyes, making it nearly impossible for her to catch her breath, let alone speak.

"I suppose we all want a family," she finally said, then wished she'd just gone for coffee instead. Wanting to fill the silence, she went on in spite of her better judgment. "I thought Steven and I would have children, of course. But we just kept putting things off—getting married, finding a home together. We couldn't even settle on a date for the wedding, and now look at me—I'm almost thirty and still as single as ever."

He did look at her, his intense inspection making her feel all warm inside, in spite of the coolness of the nearby glass.

"You still have time."

She shook her head. "Not at the rate I'm going."

He kept on looking, his smile appreciative. "You'd make a good mother."

Oh, he did have this way of just making a simple

statement sound so enticing. Maybe it was that deep, throaty voice, or the masculine little catch in his words.

"Sure," she said, her skepticism obvious. "You're just saying that to be nice."

"Right, I do tell everybody that," he countered. "In fact, I just told Maggie that in the car when she was wailing and doing her breathing exercises. And I also told Frank that he'd make a good father, and come to think of it, he was wailing, too."

"Is there something about Fairweather?" she asked, relaxing a little from his teasing.

"That makes people wail, you mean?"

She shook her head again and smiled. "No, that makes people want to settle down and produce offspring."

He tipped his head, grinning over at her. "Yeah, there's definitely something about Fairweather. This town seems to bring people together. I think it has something to do with all those adorable children we take care of in the center."

There was just a hint of promise in his words, or maybe a hint of challenge. Wanting to know more about him, she said, "How long have you been here—three years, is it?"

"Yes. But sometimes it seems as if this has always been my home, or maybe the home I was always searching for."

"Tell me about your mother," she said, turning to lean back on the windowsill. "Maggie talks about her a lot."

"My mother." He smiled, then looked down at his heavy leather ankle boots. "She comes to visit every now and then—just drops in like Mary Poppins, without warning—and she did take a liking to Maggie. She'd love to see me find just such a woman to settle down with."

So, they were back to that subject. Sara lifted off the windowsill to find the nearest chair, since she was feeling incredibly weak at the knees. Deciding to pick a safer subject to talk about while they waited, she asked him, "Ben, how...how did you find God?"

Ben's face lit up. Swinging over the chair across from her, he sat down and crossed his long legs at the ankles. "I think that was the other way around. I think God found me. My father died when I was small and my mother, Alice, was a college professor back in Madison. She tried to bring me up right, but I'm afraid I gave her a real run for her money."

Intrigued, Sara asked, "What did you do to torment your poor mother?"

He glanced out the window, rolled his neck to relieve the apparent tension centered there, then lowered his voice as he focused his attention back on Sara. "My senior year of high school, I got into some trouble. I guess I was rebelling against my lot in life—you know, no father figure and a mother who was constantly absorbed in her students and the world of academia. I fell in with the wrong crowd and got arrested for vandalism."

Sara sat up. "No! You—I can't picture you harming anyone's property."

"Well, I did. Drove around crashing mailboxes, breaking windows, stuff like that."

"Ben!"

"I know. It was terrible. Luckily though, after a night in jail, I grew up pretty fast. Out of respect for my mother, no one pressed charges."

"So, you learned your lesson and...turned to God?"

He grinned, then threw his head back against the armchair. "No, not just yet. My mother turned me in to a higher authority than herself—our minister."

"Uh-oh."

"Uh-oh is right. I was terrified of Reverend Winslow. Especially when he explained in no uncertain terms that I would be a changed teen by the end of the summer."

"Penance?"

"In a way. He put me to work in a summer camp for underprivileged inner-city kids, kids who'd never had any of the advantages I'd had. It was a real eye-opener."

"And then you found God?"

He laughed, his eyes twinkling. "Do you want to hear the whole story, or not?"

Sara ran an impatient hand through her hair. "Yes. Tell me all of it."

"As I said, God found me. Up until that time, I'd only pretended to be a Christian, mostly to keep my mother off my back. I went to church, attended youth meetings, but it was an empty, unmeaningful existence. Then that summer, I saw what it was to be a true Christian. When I got back home, I enrolled in college, but continued to do volunteer work around the church, and I worked after classes for Reverend Winslow—odd jobs and helping out with the youth. That man saved me, in more ways than one."

Sara watched his face, saw the joy in his expression. At that moment, he looked so at peace, so completely confident in his faith. She envied that. "That's a beautiful story, Ben. When did you decide to become a minister?"

"My second year in college. Went on to divinity school, then became an assistant pastor at a small church near Madison."

"I see." Sara folded her arms in her lap, and growing bolder, decided to tease him a bit. "And how about your love life? Want to tell me about that, or were you too busy to date?"

The peaceful look was shattered. His whole expression changed, and the old bittersweet sadness returned to his eyes.

"I dated in college," he told her, his tone low and cryptic. "But that's enough about me. Your turn."

Shocked at his abrupt change, she didn't know what to say. "You already know my story—and Ben, I'm sorry if I seemed to be prying."

"It's okay." But he didn't elaborate. "Go on, talk."

"I told you, you already know all about my sad state of affairs."

"Yes, I understand about that. I'm asking you, when did *you* find God?"

Sara lowered her head, then glanced back up into his eyes. He definitely wanted to change the subject, take the spotlight off himself. Not knowing what else to do or say, she obliged him. "I think maybe I haven't found Him exactly. I don't know, I was raised to believe, to have faith, but lately—"

"Then, *He'll* just have to find *you* again, same way He found me."

Sara doubted she'd have the same experience as Ben. "Does it really happen that way, you think?"

"I know," he replied, confident once again. "If you let Him in, Sara, you'll know it in your heart. You'll realize He's been right there, all along."

She sat there, watching his face, wondering again about all the many facets of Reverend Ben Hunter. There had to be more to his story, but she wouldn't push him any further tonight. Ben seemed content to let others talk, while he did all the listening. Sara had to wonder if it was a natural trait, or one borne of some long-ago pain that had caused him to shut himself away from people. Maybe because his father had died when he was so young, or maybe for some other reason. And maybe he'd tell her one day.

For now, she was content to just sit there with

him. Being near him gave her a sense of peace, of security, that she was unaccustomed to. It was a good feeling, but Sara reminded herself she couldn't get used to this.

Ben was a minister. He deserved someone who shared his same strong sense of faith. He deserved someone who had found God, not someone who couldn't even get her life in order, certainly not someone who'd just been dumped by another man because she couldn't make a firm commitment.

For the first time in a long time, Sara hoped Ben was right. She sincerely hoped God would find her again. She needed Him in her life now more than ever, to guide her through this maze of disturbing, exciting feelings she'd been bombarded with since first seeing Ben Hunter.

So she sat there, silent, smiling, and secretly asked God to show her the way, or at least to give her the strength to walk away—when the time came.

"I think it's time we had a prayer," Ben said to the group of relatives and friends of the Wrens gathered in the waiting room outside the maternity ward. Two sets of anxious grandparents-to-be got up from their chairs to stand with Ben and the others who'd come to lend their support.

Betty Anderson stood with Warren Sinclair, her soon-to-be husband, while Julianne and Luke O'Hara waited beside Rachel Talbot. Morgan, being a doctor, had gone back to check on the progress of the birth.

He came bursting through the doors then, a big smile on his face as he pulled his wife into his arms. "It's a girl. Elizabeth Anne. And she's just about perfect."

"And how are the proud parents?" someone asked.

"They are…beaming with joy," Morgan said. "Maggie came through like a trooper. And Frank, well, at least he didn't faint."

"Oh, what a relief," Betty said as she hugged Warren close. "Praise God."

Julianne smiled over at her husband. "How wonderful."

"Definitely time for a prayer," Ben reiterated.

Sara had been standing apart from the tight-knit group, not sure how to handle this. Should she join them, or just stay here and lift up her own thanks that her friend's baby was healthy?

Ben seemed to sense her hesitation. Holding out a hand, he called to her. "Sara?"

She looked into his eyes and felt as if she'd come home.

"Pray with us."

It was a statement, unflinching and unquestioning, as if he had no doubt whatsoever she'd want to be a part of this.

Sara moved into the little circle of friends and watched as they all joined hands. Humbled, she took Ben's hand in her own, acutely aware of the strength and warmth in his gentle touch. Julianne took her other hand, squeezing it briefly in an age-old symbol of understanding and camaraderie.

Then Ben's deep, emotion-packed voice filled the small waiting area.

"Lord, we thank You for the miracle of this birth, and we welcome little Elizabeth Anne Wren into the world. And we promise, as Your servants, Lord, to watch over this child, to cherish her, to teach her by example about Your great love and Your saving grace. We ask that You continue to protect her and that You continue to bless her family. We ask all of these things in Your name, Lord. Amen."

Sara looked up, her eyes misty, and found Ben's gaze centered on her face. His eyes appeared misty, too. But his smile was so rich, so promising, that she knew something wonderful was happening here tonight. Her heart picked up its tempo, her soul opened and filled with an amazing sense of happiness and fulfillment. It had been such a very long time since she'd held anyone's hand and prayed.

"Thank you." They all turned to find Frank Wren standing there in hospital scrubs, tears streaming down his rugged face. "Thanks to all of you. You all mean the world to us and we are truly blessed to have so many good friends here tonight to share in our joy."

After that, Sara stood back watching as everyone began hugging everyone else. Before she knew it, she was being hugged herself. They each pulled her close, murmuring endearments, spouting happiness. Then she looked up to find none other than Ben Hunter waiting his turn.

He pulled her close, crushing her against the scratchy wool of his navy blue sweater. She wanted to stay there forever.

Letting her go, he looked down at her. "Thanks for being here. I know it will mean a lot to Maggie."

"She's been a good friend," Sara replied on a voice thick with emotion. "I'm so happy for her."

"Tyler will have a playmate," Ben said, assurance in the statement.

"For a while at least," she replied, worried again that they'd both become too attached to the infant.

Ben glanced back down at her. "I'm beginning to think there's something to this fatherhood thing."

"Frank sure looks pleased as punch."

"It's a good night—even if we have been here for hours."

Thinking that would be a good excuse to leave before she did something crazy like cry, Sara nodded. "It is late. I guess I should get home."

"Want me to drive you?"

"That's sweet, but I have my car right outside."

Since he was still holding her, a hand on each shoulder, she didn't force herself to move. Instead, she stayed in his arms a minute longer, then said, "We'll come back and visit Maggie tomorrow, when she's rested."

"Yeah, and see that new daughter."

Sara patted him awkwardly on the back. "You'd better go get Tyler."

She watched as he nodded. "Children are a big responsibility, aren't they?"

"They certainly are."

He let her go then, but turned just as she was about to say her goodbyes to the rest of the group.

"What?" she asked, bemused by the sparkle in his eyes.

"Oh, nothing. In spite of the responsibility...I still want what they have."

With that, he glanced over at Frank, smiled and waved good-night to Sara.

"Me, too," Sara whispered later as she headed out to her car, parked near the entranceway. "Me, too."

Had God truly found her again, and brought her here to find the home and hearth she so craved? Or would she be disappointed yet again?

Or had she, in search of that elusive dream, not only found God again, but something else just as precious, too?

As she cranked her car and pulled it around, she glanced back at the wide doors leading into the hospital. Ben was there, watching her safely home.

She sighed and smiled. For so long now, it had seemed she'd been lost in the darkness, unsure which way to turn.

Maybe tonight, at long last, she'd found her way, and a light to guide her there.

Chapter Six

"**W**e need volunteers to help with the Harvest Celebration," Julianne O'Hara told Sara a week later, her brown eyes sparkling. "And I think you'd be perfect."

Sara gave her friend and fellow day-care teacher a wry smile. "I'm sure you think that. Just like you think Ben and I have a—what did you call it—a thing going on."

"Well, you do." Julianne tossed her long blond hair over her shoulder and took a sip of her hot herbal tea.

They were enjoying a quiet lunch hour while all the children took their much-needed afternoon naps. Since Sara had temporarily replaced Maggie, Julianne had taken her under her nurturing wing and they'd become fast friends. Sara enjoyed their daily luncheon chats and had grown fond of her

new friend, if not a tad envious of Julianne's glowing happiness at having found love, and an adorable
set of four-year-old twins, with Maggie's brother,
Luke.

"Oh, you're still in the newlywed stage," Sara
retorted. "You see everything with overly romantic
eyes."

Julianne leaned forward on the small table centered in the kitchen down the hall from the class-
rooms. "I can see perfectly fine, thank you."

"Yes, with rose-colored glasses."

"I don't wear glasses, but I'd have to be blind
not to notice the way Ben watches you whenever
you walk into a room. During church Sunday, I
think he wasn't preaching to anyone but you."

It had seemed that way, Sara thought now, since
he seemed to glance in her direction more times
than she cared to remember. The message, however, *had* echoed her own feelings the night Maggie
had given birth to little Elizabeth Anne.

"He's just trying to win me over to a higher
source," she replied, memories of Ben's moving
service making her smile. "He is a powerful
speaker, though."

"Yes, all that talk about walking in the light,
being children of the light—Ephesians. It was a
good sermon, but Ben seemed a bit distracted."
Her grin indicated she thought Sara was the culprit.

Sara, however, didn't want to take any credit,
even though her friend's observations hit very close
to right on the mark. "I think you're wrong. He's

probably just preoccupied because of Tyler and because Jason is still out there somewhere.''

Julianne settled back in her chair, nibbling a handful of grapes, her expression turning serious. ''You might be right. Ben takes everything to heart. He loves his congregation and he has been so worried about Jason. They were close, you know.''

Sara nodded. ''He told me. It's really a shame the Ericksons have been so stubborn about this, blaming Ben, when clearly he was only trying to help.''

''I hope that sermon got through to them,'' Julianne said. ''They sit there on the front row, acting as if they own the church, and they expect all of us to jump just because they've got so much money.'' Shrugging, she added, ''I don't mean to sound so judgmental, but they won't budge from their high-handed attitude. They need to reexamine this whole situation with Jason. Ben is not to blame here. But he insists that we all need to pray, not only for Jason, but for his parents, too.''

Sara got up to rinse her soup bowl in the sink. ''Regardless, Ben appreciates your support, I'm sure.''

Julianne finished her tea, then got up, too. ''Well, I mean it. Ben is a good person. And that's why I'm so glad you've come into his life.''

''Oh, we're back to that.''

''Mmm-hmm. Sara, he was lonely. And…well, I have to tell you a funny story. After I broke up with old what's-his-name—before I met Luke, of course—Emma tried to fix me up with Ben."

Interested in spite of herself, Sara felt a stab of jealousy. "She did?" Then she grinned. "Obviously, that match-up didn't work out."

Julianne's laughter bubbled over so loudly, she had to catch herself so she wouldn't wake the children. "It was a disaster. Don't get me wrong, Ben and I hit it off right away, but it was a brother-sister type thing. No sparks, no fast-beating hearts, just...an immediate friendship."

Julianne's description was very accurate. Sparks? Fast-beating heart? Julianne might not have fallen for Ben, but Sara had all the symptoms, all right. Glad that Ben was so brotherly to Julianne and realizing what *she* felt toward him was definitely not sisterly, Sara tried to sound sincere. "How sweet."

"You sure looked relieved."

"I'm just surprised. Ben doesn't talk about his past relationships much."

"No, I don't suppose he would," Julianne countered. "He helped me get over my fear of dating again, but he never really opened up about Nancy. Of course, Emma told me the whole story. I think she's secretly repeated it to everyone in town."

"Nancy? Who's Nancy? What story?"

"Oops." Julianne glanced around. "I shouldn't be gossiping about our minister, but you have a right to know, to understand what he went through."

Concerned but curious, Sara held up a hand. "Maybe you'd better not tell me—"

"No, let me, before Emma corners you and embellishes the whole thing. Ben met Nancy Gately in college. They were engaged and had planned to marry after Ben settled into his first church. But…three years ago, right before he came here, Nancy was killed in a car wreck on the way to work. She taught first grade, and some impatient driver pulled out right in front of her, just a few blocks away from the school."

Gasping, Sara found the nearest chair. This certainly explained Ben's reluctance to talk about his past, and it also explained the sadness that some times shrouded him. "Oh, how horrible. How horrible for Ben, and the children she taught. She must have been a very special person."

"Ben loved her so much." Julianne grabbed a tissue from her pocket and dabbed at her eyes. "I always cry when I think about what that man's been through. And after he's stood by all of us— Morgan and Rachel, Luke and me, Maggie and Frank—and soon, he'll be marrying Betty and Warren. He's always performing weddings or baptizing babies around here. That has to be so hard on him, since it's so obvious by the way he's taken to little Tyler that he'd love to have a family of his own, too."

Remembering Ben's words to her at the hospital—*I want what they have*—Sara had to clear away the lump in her throat. "And he's so gentle, so kind. He's like a rock."

"Except when it comes to his own loneliness," Julianne told her. "I think that's why Emma is constantly trying to find him the perfect partner."

Sara got back up then, her head quickly clearing. Now, more than ever, she was convinced she didn't have a future with Ben Hunter. The man was obviously still grieving over the tragedy of losing the woman he loved.

Giving her well-meaning friend a determined look, she said, "Well, none of you should pin your hopes on me. Besides the fact that I'm not cut out to be a preacher's wife, I don't know how long I'll be here and I don't know where I'm going next."

Julianne regained some of her teasing spunk then, a thoughtful expression brightening her pretty face. "Well, one day at a time, sister. I've lived here all my life and I didn't know where I was headed until I met Luke. Now I have a wonderful husband and an adorable little boy and girl to love. Ben hit it right on target with that sermon. We have to come out of the darkness sometimes."

Sara felt as if everyone in this town knew she'd had an epiphany at the hospital last week. But instead of annoying her, this only brought her a sense of comfort. "Coming here has helped me a lot, but sometimes I still feel as if I'm walking around in this heavy fog searching for…I don't know what."

Julianne drooped a slender arm across her shoulder as they walked out of the kitchen together.

"Well, high time you found your way out of that fog. And you can start by helping out with the Harvest Celebration. Oh, Sara, you'll have so much fun. We have a big fair right in the center of town—with food and crafts and artwork, music and singing. It's a great time to share our blessings and get in the mood for the holidays."

Thinking she'd need the distraction herself, Sara bobbed her head. "Okay, sign me up. I'll be glad to help out."

"Great." Julianne smiled as she scooted toward the hallway. "I'll tell Emma to put you in charge of one of the craft booths."

That should be safe enough, Sara decided as she headed back to relieve the aide watching over her sleeping babies. Surely she wouldn't have to be around Ben too much if she was busy selling pillows and quilts.

Holding a quilt that smelled faintly of baby lotion mixed with Sara's flowery perfume, Ben stood over Tyler, watching in amazement as the infant slept soundlessly in his little crib in the day-care center's nursery. Without consciously thinking about it, Ben took the whimsically patterned quilt and tucked it around the baby's chubby midsection.

"He's such a good baby," Sara said, her whisper filling the still room with a lyrical echo.

Ben turned to find her watching him. How long had she been standing there, and how was it that when she entered a room, even a room deliberately darkened for rest time, she automatically brightened everything around her? Noting the ornate silver clips that held her flaming hair off her face, and the brown wool jumper that flowed to midcalf around her slender form, he once again realized that he'd taken a keen liking to Sara Conroy.

"He has a good caregiver," he replied, waiting as she drew close. "And a pretty one, too."

"Yes, he tells me that everyday."

She didn't look at him. Instead, she kept her eyes on the baby. But Ben thought he saw a faint blush on her creamy cheeks.

"Oh, and what else does he tell you? Hope he hasn't divulged all my secrets."

He didn't miss the trace of concern, and maybe a little hesitancy, crossing her face. But the expression quickly changed to another wry smile. "I'm afraid you have no secrets, Rev. Word is out on you."

"I imagine you're right," Ben said, hoping against hope that Emma hadn't been innocently telling Sara the story of his life. Testing her, he asked, "And just what do you think you have on me, anyway?"

Sara squinted, as if debating whether to tell him or not. Then she watched as Tyler made a gurgling sound and sighed contentedly. "Oh, only that you love Emma's tea cakes, but you have to play basketball to burn up the extra calories and that you're a hardworking, considerate man who cares about your church."

Feeling anything but, Ben shrugged. "Other than my penchant for cookies, you've obviously gotten the wrong impression about me."

"Oh, no. I think I have the right impression."

Hoping to deflect some of her high praise, Ben twisted his face into a grimace. "But…that sounds so…so boring. I'm sure Tyler told you all about our dashing escapades—how we slay dragons and chase the bad guys when we're alone at home, how we help Noah build that ark all over again and follow Moses through the desert. That's why he's sleeping so hard right now. He's tuckered out from all that noble manly action."

Her laughter sounded like the wind chimes someone had hung in the picnic area out on Baylor Lake—delicate, dainty, highly feminine. Ben had to inhale to find air in the suddenly too-warm room.

"You wouldn't be telling tall tales, now, would you, Preacher?"

"Not me."

They stood silent for a moment, each looking down at the baby.

"He's so adorable," Sara said in a whisper. "How could anyone abandon something so precious?"

Ben watched the sleeping baby, then whispered an opinion. "Desperation. That's the only answer I can come up with." He reached out a hand to touch Tyler's own tiny hand. "I've been thinking…if no one comes forward to claim Tyler…I'm thinking about maybe adopting him."

Sara lifted her head, her gaze falling across Ben's face. Seeing that he was serious, she thought about what Julianne had just told her and her heart went out to him all over again. He was lonely—that much she could see. And having Tyler in his life would certainly fill that empty void Nancy's death had caused. But what if things didn't turn out the way he hoped? He'd be devastated all over again.

When she didn't answer immediately, Ben turned away from the sleeping baby, his gaze centered completely on Sara now. "You don't look so sure about what I just told you."

Glad that she was learning to think before she spoke, Sara wondered if she should tell him her doubts. "I—I just don't want you to get your hopes up. We still don't know what will happen with Tyler."

"No, but so far I'm it. I'm his only hope. And look how he's thriving. Being here, surrounded by love. He'll automatically have an extended family—a large, nurturing family. It's the best place for him."

"You might be right," she said, wishing that she could be a part of Tyler's life, too. "He's doing great and I can't think of a better place for him to be raised."

"Well, you did encourage me to take on this little task."

"Yes, I certainly did do that."

"But?"

She hated to be blunt, but it wasn't in her nature

to dance around reality. "But being a single parent might work against you, Ben. The authorities frown on that, you know."

He nodded, then scissored a hand down his face. "I've thought about all the things working against me. Short of marrying in haste, I can only hope I'd get endorsements from the congregation."

"I have no doubt about that," Sara told him. "Most of them are behind you one-hundred percent."

"But you're still not so keen on this? Why would you push me to keep him, if you don't think I have a chance of adopting him?"

Touching a hand on his arm, Sara said, "Personally, I'm very keen on you raising Tyler. I wouldn't have insisted that you take him if I didn't feel very strongly about it in my heart. I just think it would be a big responsibility, a major undertaking, to keep him for a lifetime. You work long hours and you're called out at all hours of the day and night. A lot of people depend on you already. There are so many things to consider."

"You're right." Looking defeated, he turned to leave. "Speaking of which, I have to get to the hospital right now, to check on some of my elderly church members."

Sensing his disappointment, Sara followed him. "Ben, don't give up on this. I'm sure we can weigh all the pros and cons and find a solution."

"There's only one solution as far as I'm concerned," he told her. "I want to keep Tyler with me."

After Ben left the nursery, Sara went back to stand over Tyler's crib. As much as she wanted things to work in Ben's favor, she also worried that he might be in for a fight, and that maybe, just maybe, he wanted Tyler for all the wrong reasons. Yet, she *had* been the main one to talk him into keeping the baby. If she'd known then what she knew now, she might not have insisted so much. If things fell through and he lost Tyler, he'd probably resent her for forcing him to bond with the baby, and he'd have to suffer yet another emotional loss.

Maybe she needed to examine her own motives a little better. She could have taken Tyler, yet she'd encouraged Ben to do it. Maybe because she was afraid *she'd* be the one left out in the cold? Maybe because Ben was the better choice, the strong minister with real friends who'd help him in any situation.

She'd never had that, never been a part of something so rich and so strong. Until the other night in the hospital, when she'd felt as if she truly had found a home. But that might have been a one-time deal, brought forth by an outpouring of emotion and the birth of a child. It might not happen that way again.

Yet, as she stood there, Sara couldn't help but have a little daydream of her own. For just a minute, she imagined herself in the picture with Ben and Tyler—the three of them together as a family.

But just as quickly as she conjured up that beautiful image, she pushed it away, reminding herself she didn't have what it took to be a minister's wife, and Ben might not be ready for any kind of permanent commitment. Yet...he'd said he wanted what Maggie and Frank and the rest of their friends had.

Ben wanted a family.

And so did she.

What a shame they couldn't pull it off together.

Reaching out to touch Tyler's pink cheek, she whispered, "You and the good reverend might enjoy slaying dragons and building arks, but I think I could get used to plain old boring myself."

She thought she saw Tyler smile in his sleep.

Chapter Seven

"**W**hat are you smiling about?" Sara asked Maggie a couple of weeks later as they entered the social hall of the old church.

Maggie set down the large chicken casserole she'd brought to serve at the Harvest Celebration committee meeting, her blue eyes bright with amusement.

"Oh, nothing. It's just good to see you looking so rested and relaxed. You look two shades better than when you arrived on my doorstep all those weeks ago."

Sara inclined her head and shot her friend her own smile. "Well, no wonder. Everyone around here has pampered me beyond end. Food, cards, telephone calls—I don't have time to feel sorry for myself."

"That old Minnesota spirit," Maggie replied as

she dug through a drawer for a spatula. "Or that old thing called love, maybe?"

Sara busied herself with preparing for the meeting, her head down, her gaze fixed on the counter. "Yes, this town is full of loving, caring people. A far cry from the big city."

Giving her friend a sideways glance, Maggie said, "I was referring to one particular citizen of Fairweather."

Sara stopped smiling and groaned. "Not you, too. Does everyone in this town think I'm head over heels about Ben Hunter?"

"Did I mention Ben?"

Sara blushed, then hurriedly marched to the refrigerator to pull out the liquid refreshments. "No, you didn't, but we both know that's who you were talking about. And besides, Emma has that same smile plastered on her face every time I see her, too. And she's only too happy to ask me how things are going between Ben and me, that is when she's not trying to constantly throw us together."

"Well, how *are* things going?" Maggie ignored her obvious irritation as she concentrated on heating up her casserole.

Sara found the napkins and plastic forks, then pulled out the bread and cookies she'd brought to contribute to the casual meal. "Fine. Just fine. I'm helping take care of Tyler, of course. He's the best little fellow. I see Ben at work and we talk and I see him at church and we talk and—"

"Surely there's more?" Maggie's eyes widened

as she put her hands on her hips. "What about after hours?"

"I go straight home after hours."

"Running away to the lake, huh?"

"Now, what's that supposed to mean?"

"Well, I thought you were helping Ben with Tyler, maybe even after hours. Ben needs a woman's guidance with that little boy. That child is growing so fast, and little Elizabeth Anne is right behind him. They're probably in the nursery right now, comparing formulas. And Tyler's probably whining to his new best friend that his teacher won't even come and visit after dark, simply because she's trying so hard to avoid his foster father."

That brought a smile to Sara's face, in spite of her aggravation with her friend. "I do help Ben with the baby. I take care of Tyler every day, as you well know." Shrugging, she added, "And I'm not trying to avoid anyone. Ben and I have a working agreement that we're just friends. It's best that way, keeps things in the proper perspective. We're both too caught up in our own lives to get involved with each other."

"That's not what I want to hear," Maggie admitted. "I thought surely since you'd cooked dinner for Ben that one time and you'd been so *supportive*—"

"We're friends, Maggie. That's all. And that's the way we both want it, regardless of how the rest of Fairweather feels."

Maggie gave her a mock-nasty glare. "You don't have to be so defensive."

Slamming a cookie sheet loaded with bread into the oven, along with Maggie's casserole, Sara said, "Yes, I do. Everyone keeps pushing us together and I don't think either of us is ready for that yet."

"I'm sorry," Maggie said, coming to place a hand on her arm. "I shouldn't have teased you and I didn't mean to pry."

"It's okay." Sara let out a pent-up breath, then leaned on the long serving counter. "I care about Ben—a lot. But he's still grieving over Nancy and I think he's grasping for this perfect picture of a family. I don't want him to think I can be a part of that picture."

"But why couldn't you?"

Sara scoffed, then tossed her hair back. "Look at me. I came here burned-out and tired, completely disillusioned with life. I'm not the meek-and-mild preacher's wife type. And besides, who said I wanted to be that anyway?"

"You just did," Maggie replied sagely.

"No, I didn't."

"Yes, you did. Every time you deny something so adamantly, it only means you've been thinking about that very thing."

"Oh, you sound just like you used to in college, when you were sure I had a crush on a certain boy."

"And I was usually right."

Sara had to give her that. "Well, this time you're

wrong. After Christmas, I'll be going back to St. Paul, anyway. I'm only staying on now because I want you to enjoy some time with your new baby.''

"And I appreciate that," Maggie told her. "But a lot can happen between now and Christmas."

"Not if I don't let it."

"Stubborn."

"Pushy."

Maggie nudged her good-naturedly. "Still friends?"

Sara saw the sincere expression on Maggie's serene face. Reaching out, she hugged the other woman close. "Friends forever, in spite of your overbearing interference in my private life." Patting Maggie on the back, she grudgingly added, "And...thanks for caring."

"Always." Maggie smiled a bit too smugly. Then, as the other committee members started arriving, she busied herself with laying out the food.

Emma pranced in, resplendent in teal wool, followed by Betty Anderson with her daughter, Rachel Talbot, and Julianne O'Hara. In a few minutes, the other church members who'd volunteered to help had arrived and the meeting was about to get started.

"We're expecting one more person," Emma stated as she gathered her folders and charts, a practiced smile encasing her pink lips.

Just then Ben walked into the room and nodded a greeting to all the people gathered around the long table, his gaze locking on Sara as he stood over the group.

Bidding her heart to slow down, Sara glanced up at him, hoping she didn't look as lovesick as she felt. Since everyone in the room was watching her, she gave a shaky little wave of the hand, tore her eyes away from the man who'd somehow managed to ingratiate himself into her whole being, then quickly looked down at the table in front of her.

"Hi, there, Reverend Ben," Emma said, beaming up at him. "We were just about to get started. I'll pass out your assignment sheets, then we'll eat Maggie's good-smelling casserole while we go over the details."

"Great," Ben said as he found a chair near Sara. "I'm starving."

Emma handed him a stack of papers. "Take one and pass them along." Then she gave a dainty shrug and sent Ben and Sara one of her best Strawberry Queen smiles. "Oh, and by the way, I've assigned you two to the craft booth. Hope you don't mind a four-hour shift together."

"Have you been avoiding me?" Ben asked Sara later as he bundled little Tyler, who'd just been handed over by a nursery worker, into his stroller and secured him with a thick blanket.

Because of Emma's fast-paced meeting agenda, they'd had little time for any personal conversation, but the meeting was over now and everyone was ready to go home.

Sara glanced around to make sure the others weren't listening. Emma and Betty were deep in conversation with Rachel, and Julianne was holding little Elizabeth Anne and helping Maggie clean up. Most of the other members had left.

"I don't think so," she began, careful not to look at him for fear he'd see she wasn't being exactly honest. "We see each other every day."

Ben shot her a dubious look. "True. But you seem to be in such a hurry all the time. What happened to all those interesting conversations we had when you first came here?"

"Haven't we been communicating?"

"Depends on your definition of 'communicating.'"

Nervous and cornered, Sara tried not to squirm. Helping him to put on Tyler's bright red winter hat, she said, "Did you need to ask me something specific?"

Ben finished dressing the baby, then stood. "Yes. Why are you avoiding me?"

Pushing at her wayward curls, she gave him what she hoped was an honest look. "I've just been so busy—with work and…things. I've been going by to check on Maggie and give her some relief. Newborns can wear you out and new mothers need their rest."

"Yeah, I know all about newborns," Ben countered, his expression quizzical as he nodded toward wide-eyed Tyler.

"Do you think I've been neglecting you and Tyler?"

"Yes. Horribly. But I intend to make up for that. How about dinner soon? My place. I don't think I've ever told you, but I can cook a mean pot of Texas-style chili."

"Chili?" Sara laughed then, and immediately relaxed back into the old familiar banter. "Have you ever been anywhere near Texas?"

"No, but I have lots of reliable cookbooks. My mother gives me one just about every birthday— thinks a bachelor needs to learn to cook for himself."

"I have to meet your mother. She sounds like such a sensible woman."

"I'd like for you to meet my mother."

The banter was gone, replaced with something as warm and alluring as a mug of rich hot chocolate. The way he'd said that, his tone low and gravelly, promising and wistful all at the same time, told Sara that she'd just stumbled back into dangerous territory.

Hoping to get out safely again, she bobbed her head, then started collecting her stuff. "That would be nice."

"She usually comes for the Harvest Celebration. And she always comes for Christmas, since that's my busy season and it's hard for me to get away to go visit her."

"Then I look forward to seeing her."

"What about dinner?"

"Sure, I'd love to have dinner with your mother sometime."

"No, I mean, yes, that would be great. But what about my chili?"

Her immediate reaction was to make an excuse, but her heart wouldn't allow her to do that. So she caved in. "Is this chili safe for human consumption?"

"Barely, but that's beside the point."

She grinned then. "Oh, and just what is the point, Rev?"

"I miss you."

Sara had to swallow and catch her breath. Eating chili was now the farthest thing from her mind, but she did feel as if she'd gotten hold of some fire. Maybe it was the way he stood there, looking at her with those beautiful, poetic blue eyes, or maybe it was the way his voice carried to her ears only, so intimate, so cozy, so appealing.

"I haven't gone anywhere," she finally managed to say.

"Then it's a date?"

"When?"

"How about this Saturday? We can start early, maybe enjoy a walk in the last of the fall leaves before we head in to eat some spicy chili?"

That would mean two Saturdays in a row with Ben, since Emma had given them the Saturday late shift at the celebration, too.

Searching for excuses to decline, she asked,

"What about Tyler?" At least the baby would be a source of distraction.

"He can't eat chili just yet."

"No, I mean will he come along on this excursion through the leaves? It is awfully chilly some afternoons now. I could stay in with him, if you feel the need to kick up some leaves."

He shook his head. "Why would I want to go for a walk by myself? I'm sure he'll want a front-row seat, with me doing all the stroller pushing."

She giggled in spite of herself, then came up with another stalling technique. "And what do you plan on doing with him during the Harvest Celebration the next Saturday? Will he be okay while we work? If not, I can stay with him and arrange for you to have another booth partner."

"Sadie has the nursery shift that day."

Sara liked Sadie Fletcher, an older African-American church member who'd raised six children and was now working on spoiling about twice as many grandchildren—most of whom also stayed at the center. Sadie worked part-time in the day-care center and helped out with the church nursery on Sunday mornings, too. She was famous for her hugs and grandmotherly wisdom. And the children adored her. No way to change that arrangement.

Deflated, she said, "Oh, then he'll be just fine."

"And so will you," Ben told her, his expression quizzical. "You're out of excuses, Sara, so don't look so glum."

"I'm not glum. I'm just relieved to hear Sadie will be taking care of him. She loves Tyler."

"Everyone loves little Tyler," Ben replied, smiling down at the alert infant.

Glad to shift the subject matter away from her, Sara quickly agreed. "He's growing so fast."

"He is pretty amazing. But I worry that he gets passed around so much with all these sitters and day-care. You were right about that, but like most working parents, I don't have much choice." He ran a hand down Tyler's pink cheek. "To make up for leaving him so much, I just enjoy sitting at night and holding him."

Good. She'd diverted his attention away from their chili-cooking, leaf-tossing possible day together. Fortified, she kept talking about the baby instead.

"I'm sure he loves being held. And I think that's an important part of being a working parent. You have to spend quiet time with your children, let them know you love them."

As they headed out the door, Ben turned to lock things up. Everyone else had somehow managed to scoot, leaving them alone. A cold blast of air greeted them on the way to the parking lot. "Well, I'm just so blessed that we have one of the best day-care centers in the area right here at The Old First Church. Doubly blessed, since I get to visit with him and you at the same time."

Sara chose to ignore that sweet remark. She couldn't afford to encourage this relationship, even though she reminded herself, she'd just agreed to having another cozy meal with Ben and Tyler. Thinking maybe she should come up with a more plausible excuse so she could refuse, she opened her mouth to speak.

But as she watched Ben fussing over the baby, the words died on her lips. She *wanted* to eat chili and walk through golden leaves with these two. She wanted to spend quiet time with them, away from the hustle and bustle of the nursery and Ben's hectic work schedule. She wanted to get to know Ben better, away from prying eyes and teasing remarks. She wanted these things in her heart, even while her head told her she shouldn't ask for them. So she just stood there, freezing.

Ben checked Tyler to make sure he was warm, then lifted the collar of his quilted jacket. "Winter's coming."

"That's for sure."

He walked with Sara to her car, then turned as she bent to open the door, a hand on her arm. "Sara, are you avoiding me because you don't agree that I should try to adopt Tyler? It does seem as if your attitude changed once I told you I was considering it."

The doubt in his question, and his misunderstanding as to why she'd pulled back from him, tore through her. She couldn't lie to this man, she couldn't hide what was in her heart. It wouldn't be fair to either of them.

"Ben...I didn't realize I was avoiding you.

Okay, maybe I was being standoffish. I guess I just thought we both needed some time."

"Was I coming on too strong?"

"No, not at all. You've been such a good friend, but…it's important that we both understand that's all we can be. I just thought it best if I gave you and Tyler some breathing room."

He reached out to pull a strand of hair off her chin. "But we like having you around. Tyler talks about you all the time."

Sara lifted her head, the warmth of his finger brushing her cheek like a touch of flame against the bitter cold. "What does Tyler say about me?"

He leaned closer then, his eyes holding hers in the glowing security light from the churchyard. "That you always have a smile for him, that you smell like a spring garden, that your hair is full of sunshine and autumn, that your voice is as soft as a song."

Gulping in a breath, she whispered, "That Tyler sure has a way with words. Have you been reading poetry to him?"

"He's a very smart little fellow. And yes, sometimes late at night when we can't sleep, we read…everything from the Bible to Robert Frost or *The Odyssey*. Or I play the guitar and sing off-key to him. He kicks up his heels to 'Just a Closer Walk with Thee,' but I think he really prefers 'Just As I Am.' He gets wide-eyed with excitement, just listening to the possibilities of life."

Sara had to hide her sigh. A poetic, guitar-playing preacher who sang lullabies to an orphaned baby. Did she really think she stood a chance against these two?

Trying to sound rational and unaffected, she tugged on Tyler's wool booty. "Well, he certainly looks wide-awake right now." She leaned down toward the baby, just to distract herself from the sweet image of these two sitting by a fire, taking a literary adventure to heart. "But I can't resist giving him a good-night kiss." She did just that, laughing as the baby gurgled, before she turned to get in her car.

"Not so fast." Ben whirled her back around, his hand cupping her chin. Before she could take another breath, he gave her a quick peck on the mouth. "I couldn't resist giving *you* a good-night kiss."

With that, he let her go, stepped back, then grinned. "I'll see you Saturday—come hungry."

Sara didn't think that would be a problem. She yearned for a taste of something, but she didn't think food had anything to do with whatever it was.

Touching a hand to her lips, she watched as Ben walked the baby stroller the few blocks to his own house. Then she thought she heard him whistling, but it might have just been the wind.

Ben heard the phone ringing even as he jingled his keys in the front door. Pushing the stroller inside, he rushed to pick up the receiver, catching it on the fourth ring.

"Hello?"

"Reverend Ben?"

The voice was shaky and far-away sounding, but Ben recognized it immediately. "Jason?"

"It's me. How are things?"

"How are *you,* Jason? Where are you calling from?"

"That doesn't matter. I just…I just needed to hear a familiar voice."

Ben pulled Tyler's stroller along, then sat down in the armchair by the silent fireplace, one hand rocking the stroller to appease the infant as he tried to talk to the teenager. "Jason, why don't you come home? Your parents are so worried about you."

"Yeah, I'm sure."

"They are," Ben said, stressing the words. "I just talked to your father a few weeks ago. Why don't you call him?"

"No."

"Jason, you can't make it out there alone, especially with winter setting in. Let me help you."

"No, I just called to see how things are going with you. How's the team doing?"

Ben shifted, his head lowered. "The team's okay. We could use a good center, though."

"And the practices—are you still having regular practices?"

Hoping to hold him on the line, so he'd open up, Ben thought about all the familiar, everyday things he could tell Jason. "Well, yes. I've had to do some major juggling, though. Jason, you won't believe it, but someone left a baby in the church—about a month ago. A cute little boy. And I'm taking care of him.''

Ben heard a sharp intake of breath, then silence. ''Jason, are you still there?''

''Yes, sir. A baby? Wow. Do—do you know who the baby belongs to?''

''No. We can't seem to locate the parents, so we got it cleared for me to be his foster parent. I'm thinking about adopting him, though.''

''You are?''

Hoping that talking about his own struggles would help the boy share his problems, Ben continued. ''Yes. His name is Tyler and he's so beautiful, or handsome, I guess I should say. He has this bright fuzz of reddish-blond hair and big blue-green eyes. And he has the hands of a true basketball player.''

Silence, then, ''Sounds like you care about him a lot.''

''I do. I sure do. He's both a blessing and a challenge.''

Silence again.

''Jason?''

''Sir?''

''I could use some help—you know, someone to pinch-hit when I get busy. Why don't you come home and meet Tyler?''

''No. I can't do that.''

Surprised at how shaky the boy sounded, Ben

hoped he might be reaching Jason at last. "Why not?"

"Just can't."

Ben heard a sniffling sound. Tears misted over in his own eyes while he gripped the phone so hard, he was sure it would crack. "Jason, son, I've been praying for you to stay safe. And I'm praying that you'll find your way home. Do you hear me?"

"Uh-huh." More sniffles.

"Tell me where you are. I'll come and get you."

"No. Just...just take care of that baby, okay?"

There was a loud click, then the suspended silence of the dial tone ringing in Ben's ear.

He put the phone down, feeling more alone there in the darkness then he ever had in his life. Then he heard little Tyler gurgling.

Wanting more than anything to hold the child close, Ben lifted the baby out of his protective blankets and gently cradled the tiny bundle in his arms.

"Lord, please help Jason," he said into the night. "Winter's coming and he's out there, alone and frightened. Help him, Lord, to know that no matter what he's done, no matter the burden, You will bring him comfort and forgiveness. Bring Jason back to us, God. Bring him back to us safe and sound. I ask this in Your name. Amen."

Ben sat there for a long time, cooing to Tyler, then praying to God. He was afraid to let the baby go, afraid to put him down in his little crib. So he just sat there, holding on while Tyler took a bedtime bottle, then drifted off into a deep, peaceful sleep.

"Why can't we all sleep so peacefully?" Ben asked, his voice carrying out over the still night.

He looked around at his home. Rat lay curled on the couch, oblivious to any human suffering. And two more cats, aptly named Calico and Chubby, lay sprawled on the braided rug, probably wondering in their dreams why Ben hadn't come home to build them a cozy fire tonight.

Safe. Ben and his menagerie were safe.

He only wished he could feel the same way about Jason.

Exhausted, he finally got up to put Tyler to bed. As he stood over the little boy, he made a promise.

"I won't ever let that happen to you."

He hoped, prayed that God would see fit to help him live up to that promise. Now, more than ever, he realized the tremendous responsibility of raising a child. But he still wanted that responsibility; he still wanted to adopt Tyler.

Ben gave the baby a gentle kiss, then he went back into the sitting room and, clasping his hands together, he started praying all over again.

Chapter Eight

The next morning, after dropping Tyler off in the nursery, Ben hurried back to his office to call Richard Erickson. He dreaded making the call, but he had to do it. Regardless of their feelings toward Ben, the Ericksons needed to know that Jason was safe.

Mary Erickson answered on the second ring. "Hello?"

Ben cleared his throat and sent up a prayer. It was always hard, talking to them about Jason. "Mrs. Erickson, this is Reverend Ben Hunter. Can I come over to visit with you and Mr. Erickson before he leaves for the office?"

"Why? What's this about? Is it Jason?"

Hearing the panic in the woman's voice, Ben quickly reassured her. "Yes. I heard from him again, late last night. I thought you'd want to know."

"Of course."

She was sobbing so hard, Ben hardly heard her response. His heart went out to her. "I'll be over in about five minutes."

The phone clicked in his ear.

"Emma, I'm going to talk to the Ericksons," he said as he rushed past the startled secretary who'd just arrived for work. "I might be a while."

Emma bobbed her head in understanding. "I'll say a prayer for all of you."

"Good. We need it. Especially Jason. I'm very worried about him."

"Did you hear from him again?"

"Yes, late last night. He didn't sound so good, either."

Emma got up then, halting him with an waving hand. "I'm not one to spread gossip, as you know, but I heard something interesting the other day when I went to visit my sister in New Hope. I just forgot to tell you about it. I knew there was something important I needed to tell you."

Trying to be patient, Ben stopped at the door. "Emma, can this wait?"

Not in the least affronted, Emma said, "It's about Jason."

"What?"

"You remember that youth trip way back last year? The one where you took the kids to New Ulm during spring break?"

"Yes, I remember."

"Well, according to my sister, several of the

youth from her church there in New Hope also went on the trip.''

Ben nodded, wishing Emma could tell a story faster. ''Yes, about four area churches brought their youth that weekend.''

''Okay, well, one of the girls from Bertha's— that's my sister—have you ever met her—she's my *older* sister...''

''Yes, I think I have,'' Ben said, his hand moving to indicate she needed to bring things to a wrap.

''Anyway, Bertha said this young girl named Patty Martin—Mitchell, something like that—went on the outing with their youth. She wasn't a member, rarely came to youth meetings, but she went along on the trip. Well, apparently she took a liking to a boy from Fairweather—said his name was Jason.''

Ben dissected what Emma was trying to tell him. ''Patty met Jason Erickson on this youth trip?''

''I think so,'' Emma replied, bobbing her tightly bunned head. ''But from what Bertha told me, I don't think his parents knew about the relationship.''

Wanting to hear more, but concerned that the Ericksons were waiting, Ben waved his hand again. ''What are *you* trying to tell *me*, Emma?''

''Well, Bertha and I got to comparing notes— you know about things that have happened recently—just talking, worrying, you understand.''

''Yes, I understand,'' Ben said, his patience walking a thin line. ''What did Bertha say?''

"Bertha said that Patty Martin ran away from home at around the same time Jason Erickson did."

Emma stopped for dramatic effect, her words knocking the wind right out of Ben's body.

"Do you think they ran away together?"

"I'm not suggesting that," Emma replied, holding up a hand, "but it does seem a mighty big coincidence, don't you think?"

"Mighty big," Ben had to agree. This certainly added a new wrinkle to the whole sad situation. Yet Jason had never mentioned this girl. "If this is the case, why haven't we heard about Patty before? Jason certainly hasn't mentioned being with anyone."

Emma clucked her tongue. "Patty Martin comes from a very troubled home—very poor. Apparently she's been in and out of trouble a lot. Her parents didn't even bother reporting her missing until months after she'd left. Said she'd done this before, but she always came back home. Just recently, her mother happened to confide in one of the women at the church that Patty had been secretly seeing a very wealthy boy from Fairweather—Jason, of course, and that he was the reason she ran away. Now Bertha says everyone in New Hope is talking about it, so naturally when we started putting two and two together—"

"Naturally," Ben finished, pinching the bridge of his nose with his forefinger and thumb, the beginnings of a headache working its way through his throbbing brain. "Sounds as if you and Bertha need to open a detective business on the side." Shaking his head, he added, "As for this girl's parents, honestly, I don't understand some people. They should have reported this immediately."

"Pray for them," Emma said. "From what I gather, they said good riddance to the girl." Giving a long-suffering sigh, she sat back down to get her workday started.

Ben envied Emma. She was so innocent, so content to do her work and help out here and there, and provide much-needed information in the giddy form of harmless gossip. She had no way of knowing that what she'd just told him would only add to the Ericksons' woes.

As far as Ben could tell, they'd never approved of any of Jason's friends. It wouldn't help matters to tell them that their son might have run away with a girl they didn't even know, a girl from what they would obviously term the wrong side of the tracks.

But how had he missed this? Ben wondered as he drove the short distance to the Ericksons' mansion. Thinking back, he didn't remember Jason hanging out with any one particular person on that spring retreat. But then, there had been well over fifty teenagers milling around on the scheduled tours of the quaint, historical town. It had taken all he and the other chaperones could do just to keep up.

I should have been more aware, he told himself as he pulled his utility vehicle up the winding drive to the Ericksons' gabled Victorian house. They'd blame him for this, too, he was sure.

And they'd be right to lay blame at his feet.

"I don't believe you," Richard Erickson said a few minutes later, after Ben had told him about his conversation with Emma. "My son would never run away with a girl he barely knows. That's just not like Jason."

Mary, a petite woman with a soft brown pixie haircut, glanced at her husband, her dark eyes red-rimmed and watery. Then she turned back to Ben. "Did...did he ever mention this Patty to you?"

"No, ma'am," Ben told the heartbroken woman. "He's never mentioned anything about being with another person."

"It's all just a pack of lies," Richard said, jumping up off the sofa in the formal living room to pace before the enormous marble fireplace. "Emma needs to learn not to listen to idle gossip."

"I couldn't agree with you more," Ben pointed out, "but she's only trying to help. I intend to go to New Hope and ask the minister there if this could be true. If you'd like, I'll talk to the girl's parents, too."

Mary looked across at him then. "That would certainly help to ease our minds, Reverend. Thank you."

Ben looked around at the house, wondering how any child could have a normal life in such a place. It was beautiful, full of priceless antiques and imported luxuries that had somehow survived centuries of Ericksons, yet it seemed to be missing that lived-in look most modern homes had. Everything about the Erickson household was stilted and formal, with no hope for straying away from that theme. And tiny Mary Erickson worked day and night to keep things proper for her demanding husband.

Sensing that Jason's mother needed his guidance, in spite of her husband's hostility, Ben nodded, then took her hand in his. "Mrs. Erickson, I will do whatever it takes to bring Jason home. I promise you that."

She clutched his hand as if it were a lifeline. "You were good to our boy. I don't think I ever thanked you for that."

"You don't need to thank him!" Richard shouted, a shocked expression on his face. "Have you forgotten that this man instigated the changes in our son? Jason was fine until we got a new minister. Reverend Olsen would have never encouraged Jason the way Hunter here has."

Mary let go of Ben's hand then to stare up at her husband. "Reverend Olsen is a good, decent man, but he had lost touch with the young people in our church."

"How can you say that?"

"I'm not disrespecting him," Mary said on a timid voice, "but you can't deny that since Ben came here, our youth program has grown."

"That's because he lets them get away with foolish things. He encourages them in all the wrong areas.''

Richard Erickson glared down at Ben, clearly intent on believing the worst. And right now, Ben had to agree with him. But he couldn't let that get in the way of helping Jason.

Ben stood then, a hand raised in the air to ward off any more attacks. ''I'm not here to defend myself. I'm certainly not perfect, and I'll never be able to fill Reverend Olsen's shoes, but I love your son. I love all of the teenagers, the children, in my congregation. Right now, my only concern is to help Jason. Can we all agree on that, at least?''

Mary nodded her head, then reached for a fresh tissue. ''Whatever you can do, Reverend, I'd appreciate it.''

Richard didn't look so sure. Finally, with a defeated sigh, he sat back down on the sofa, his head caught in his hands. ''I miss my son, Reverend. I've used every means available to try and find him, but I'm losing hope.''

Ben reached out a hand to touch Richard Erickson's coat sleeve. ''I understand, sir. And from what I've seen and read about teenage runaways, they go underground and watch out for each other by turning their backs on adults. Jason is out there somewhere, hiding away for some reason, and so far he's ignoring all our pleas and our efforts to help him. But I'm asking you not to give up hope. As long as Jason keeps calling me, we can know he's safe and I'll encourage him to seek help. Until he's ready to come home, I'll do whatever I can to help track him down."

Mr. Erickson didn't pull away as he'd expected. Instead, he placed a shaking hand over Ben's, his eyes bright with tears he couldn't shed. "I'll hold you to that promise, Reverend."

Ben lowered his head, then gave the other man a direct stare. "I promise. And I don't want you to give up on me, either. I'm still struggling here, each and every day, and I'll be the first to admit I've made some mistakes. But I've always had the best intentions regarding the children within this church. I want you to know that and…I need your prayers and your support."

His words and his request seemed to filter through some of Richard Erickson's disapproval. The harsh planes of the older man's features softened ever so slightly. But he remained silent, his eyes still wary and uncertain.

"I'm counting on you," Mary offered. "And I'll pray for you, too." Then she got up to come and sit by her husband, giving him a pleading look. "Richard, could we stop blaming Reverend Hunter and work on seeking help for our son—together, the three of us?"

Richard's nod was slow and hesitant, but Ben could tell the man didn't have anywhere else to turn.

"Let's pray," Ben suggested.

With that, Mary placed her hand over her husband's, then reached out to Ben. "Reverend?"

Ben put his hand over their clasped ones, then turned to the Lord for the answers they all sought...

A few minutes later, he left the Ericksons', feeling as if he'd just somehow survived a very hard-fought test. Now he had to live up to the promises he'd just made.

And he would—somehow.

"I appreciate you going with me," Ben told Sara as they headed out of town toward New Hope.

It was a brilliant, cold but sunny Saturday morning, making the unpleasant trip bearable at least.

"I don't mind a bit," Sara told him, turning in her seat to check on little Tyler. The baby was happily kicking in his snug car seat. "This is just all so very sad."

Ben's face reflected that sadness.

He'd told her all about the entire situation late yesterday afternoon, when he'd come by to pick up Tyler. And before she'd been able to stop herself, Sara had volunteered to ride over to New Hope with him, to find some possible answers to all his questions regarding Jason and Patty.

Now she was glad she'd insisted on coming along. Yesterday he seemed to be carrying the weight of the world on his broad shoulders, and today he wasn't much better. He definitely needed a friend, and since most of his male buddies were now happily married and busy with their new families, that left Sara.

Again, she had to wonder if God had brought

her to Fairweather for just such a reason. But that would be too much to ask—finding the perfect man in the perfect little town. And a baby to love, too.

I won't get my hopes up, she told herself as she glanced out at the rolling Minnesota countryside. She'd just concentrate on lending Ben support and encouragement, to help him through this rough spot. Besides, she didn't want to spoil this nice drive by fretting over her place in this world.

"I just about missed fall," she stated now, hoping to keep the conversation light. "Look at those trees. There is nothing like fall in Minnesota."

All around them, the brilliant orange, russet, gold and brown of fall lifted out, the trees so thick with foliage they looked like a patterned quilt.

Ben kept his eyes on the road, but nodded. "Yeah, and I'm just sorry I had to cancel our walk."

"That's okay. Driving's just as nice. It's breathtaking."

He lifted his head. "It's a shame we have to even make this trip. I wish I could make Jason see that he needs to come home."

Sara looked over at Ben's profile, well aware that he wasn't even seeing the glorious tapestry spread out around them. His face showed the strain of worrying about the runaway. "Did you get any sleep last night?"

"Not really." He chanced a glance at her, then brought his attention back to the curving road. "I—

I just feel somehow responsible for all of this. I've gone over everything in my mind, but—"

"It's not your fault, Ben," she told him, wishing there was a way she could help him believe that. "I mean, you're only one man, and you've tried to be the best counselor, the best example a man could be to the youth in your church."

"But that's just it—I'm supposed to lead the members of my church, set an example for them. What if I set the wrong example? What if I did put ideas into Jason's head?"

"By offering him guidance and friendship, by teaching him how to be a better basketball player?" Sara shook her head, causing the hood of her parka to shift against the seat. "No, I'm telling you—I believe you did the best you could. Isn't that all any of us can ever do?"

Ben's smile didn't lift the darkness in his eyes. "Thank you," he said, his gaze falling across her face.

Giving him a sideways glance, she said, "For what?"

"For believing in me."

Suddenly aware that she'd been a bit fierce in her defense of him and his obvious abilities, Sara glanced back out the window. But she wasn't embarrassed; she did believe in Ben. As any friend would. "And why shouldn't I?"

He shrugged. "That's the part I don't get. You aren't even a member of my church—yet. But you seem to have more faith in me than a lot of my own church members.''

Realizing she was slipping back into the danger zone, Sara shrugged back at him. ''You know, I worked in a big city hospital for several years. I saw all kinds of people coming through those doors—all kinds of parents, good and bad, some caring and loving, some uncaring and brutal. It forced me to become a very good judge of character.'' She was silent for a minute, then she added, ''And it made me cynical and jaded, too. I came here with an attitude. I was broken, tired, disillusioned in both spirit and body.''

''But now?''

''But now, I—I feel better every day.'' She swallowed, held her breath, then said what was in her heart. ''And—you're part of the reason I can say that now.''

He looked surprised, but pleased. ''I've helped you?''

''You've helped me. So you see, you aren't so bad.''

''Maybe not.''

''I know not.''

''Does this mean you *really do* like being with me?''

She liked the genuine smile breaking across his face to erase the worry lines she'd noticed earlier. But she wasn't about to admit anything close to her true feelings. ''This means I'm willing to eat your chili.''

"It's a start," he told her, his eyes holding hers. "If we get back home in time for me to cook it."

"If not, we'll just grab a burger," she told him.

"Now Tyler might go for that. I think he's just about ready to move up to some solid food soon."

"He does have an appetite."

As if knowing they were discussing him, Tyler made a gurgling giggle, then kicked his booties high in the air.

Sara laughed, turning to grab a kicking little foot. "You are so adorable, and you know it, don't you?"

The baby gave her a toothless grin, then in typical baby fashion, settled back with droopy eyes to take a little nap.

Sara had never felt so content, so settled herself. This could be habit-forming, this hanging out with Ben and Tyler. Her heart lurched strangely at the thought of having to leave them and go back to the city. But soon...

She decided not to dwell on that right now. This day was too beautiful for regrets and worry.

All around them, golden leaves emerged over the narrow road to form a brilliant canopy. The sky was a rich, promising blue.

Too promising. Too hopeful. Sara sat back in her corner of the sturdy vehicle, afraid to cast a glance over at Ben for fear he'd see what was in her heart. This shouldn't feel so right, so good. But it did.

So she enjoyed the silence, the soft music from

the radio and Ben's soft gaze on her face each time she glanced up at him.

A few minutes later, however, they pulled into the parsonage near the church where Emma's sister was a member. Ben had arranged to talk to the pastor at home.

"Okay, here we go," he said as he shut off the engine. "Maybe we can find out something about Jason and Patty."

"I'll watch Tyler," Sara told him. "I'll push him around the yard in his stroller while you talk to the pastor."

"Okay, but don't get too chilly."

"We'll be fine," she assured him. "He's all bundled up and the sun's out."

Ben helped her with the baby's stroller, then headed to the wooden-framed white house while she cooed to the now wide-awake baby. Then he turned at the steps.

"Sara?"

"Hmmm?"

"Nothing. I'm just glad you came."

"Me, too," she told him as she urged him on.

Ben knocked on the heavy wooden door, then stepped back to wait. An older man came out on the porch, then smiled and shook Ben's hand.

"I'm Reverend Harry Brooks. Glad to meet you at last, Ben. I've heard good things about your church in Fairweather."

"Thanks," Ben said. "I appreciate your agreeing to meet with me."

"No problem." Reverend Brooks glanced out toward Sara and Tyler, his smile as warm as the sunshine. Then he nudged Ben on the arm. "Well, son, don't make your pretty wife and that cute little one stay out in the cold. Bring them on in by the fire."

Sara watched as a surprised Ben turned from the polite minister to her. Something in his eyes caught at her soul and held her there, like a freeze frame from a movie.

In that gentle, coaxing voice she knew so well, she heard him say, "Maybe it is time they both came in out of the cold."

With that, he motioned for her.

Sara had no choice but to follow him into the house.

She noticed he didn't bother correcting Reverend Brooks. He didn't tell the man that she wasn't his wife and Tyler wasn't his child.

So she did. "I'm just a friend—Sara Conroy—and this is little Tyler. We're taking care of him…for someone else."

"What a pity," Reverend Brooks said, shaking his salt-and-pepper head. "You three look like you belong together."

Sara didn't have to look up to see what Ben was thinking. She could feel it in the way he was watching her.

And she wondered how such an innocent assumption, coming from a complete stranger, could feel so wonderful and so painful all at the same time.

Chapter Nine

"Okay, so we know that Patty Martin left home at the same time Jason Erickson did."

Ben stood over the stove at Sara's cottage, absently stirring the bubbling chili he's spent the better part of the hour putting together. His mind whirled and bubbled just like the hearty mix he'd fixed for dinner. Now he wasn't so sure he could even eat the chili. Somehow, over the course of the afternoon, he'd managed to lose his appetite.

"Yes." Sara nodded beside him as she finished up the salad she'd created for the meal. "And we now know that what Emma told us was true—Patty and Jason had some sort of relationship going on."

"A secret relationship," Ben replied, picking up a dish towel to wipe his hands. "How am I supposed to tell the Ericksons that their son had been writing letters to this girl, meeting with her on weekends, sending her e-mails? How do I tell them that Jason had fallen in love, but felt forced to keep that love a secret from his own parents?''

"It won't be easy."

"No, especially when you compare the two families."

They'd also gone by the address Reverend Brooks had given them to see if they could talk to Patty's parents. The rundown little house was a testament to a gloomy existence, and Patty's parents hadn't given them much hope. They'd been tight-mouthed and condemning about their daughter, and didn't seem in the least concerned about her whereabouts.

"She'll turn up when she gets tired of having too much fun," Fred Martin had told them, a cigarette dangling from his cracked lips. "She thought she'd hit pay dirt this time, though. A rich boy." With that, the man had huffed, coughed, then turned to go back into the dilapidated house.

His wife, who worked as a cashier at a nearby convenience store and looked aged beyond her forty or so years, hadn't offered much hope, either. "We did everything we could for Patty, but she was too hardheaded to listen to us. I was married and had babies by the time I was her age. She'll learn soon enough."

Ben had gotten the impression that Patty's mother had suffered more than she'd let on herself. He didn't want to call it abuse, but both he and Sara had noticed the bruises lining the woman's skinny arms. He had to wonder if that was one of the reasons Patty had left home.

"I don't think Patty has had much positive reinforcement," Sara said now, shaking her head in wonder. "We never know how lucky we are to have good, solid parents until we're too old to appreciate it, do we?"

Ben shook his head. "I'd like to know the whole story regarding that family, though. I'm glad Reverend Brooks is keeping an eye on Patty's mother, for her own safety."

"Yes, but there's only so much he can do. Mrs. Martin will have to be the one to get away, if she is being abused. That could explain why Patty left, at least."

Ben stood silent for a minute, making a mental note to stay in touch with Reverend Brooks to see what else they could do. It had been a long day and he was exhausted, soul-weary. But at least he was with Sara now. She certainly brightened the gloom surrounding their mission.

He watched as Sara finished up her handiwork then put away the rest of the lettuce and other salad fixings, enjoying the way she hummed when she sliced cucumbers, enjoying the way her long wool skirt swished around those adorable flat-heeled boots she liked to wear.

He was so very glad she'd gone with him today.

She'd been right there, by his side, coaxing Reverend Brooks, asking the questions Ben couldn't seem to voice when they'd come face to-face with

Patty's parents. She'd helped him through this, and now they were back here, at her little house, watching as dark clouds rolled in out over Baylor Lake while Tyler slept peacefully in his portable bed nearby. It had been her idea to come here to fix dinner.

"The lake has a way of soothing your soul," she'd told him on the way back to Fairweather.

So a couple of hours ago, they'd picked up the necessary supplies and headed out here. With a few minutes of daylight left and the earlier sunny day being replaced by what promised to be a winter storm, Sara had urged Ben out the door. "Go take a long walk, and relax. I'll feed Tyler and get him to sleep for you."

She'd been right, of course. The lake waters had glistened like teardrops underneath the looming gray-blue clouds, and Ben had had a long talk with God, asking, hoping, praying for guidance and strength.

Sara was good for him, Ben decided as he watched her going about her work. She made him see things so much more clearly. He was beginning to depend on her.

Now she turned to give him her complete attention, and his heart did that little dance that it always did whenever he went into the day-care center to visit with Tyler. His Sara dance—a little flutter of beating pulse that only she could bring out. He had to hold his heart in check, just to hear what she was saying to him.

"Ben, you have to be honest with the Ericksons. You owe them that. They won't like hearing what we found out, but at least they'll know Jason isn't out there alone."

"I know," he replied, wishing they had a better topic of conversation, "but it's only going to hurt them worse. They didn't have a clue—none of us did—that Jason and Patty were serious about each other. Certainly not serious enough to run away together."

"When it comes to teenagers, who does have a clue?" she asked, throwing her hands up. "You remember being one, don't you?"

He gave her a sheepish grin then. "Oh, yeah. I gave my mother lots of sleepless nights. And I'm amazed I didn't do something stupid like run away myself."

Sara bobbed her head in agreement. "Me, too. My mother and I used to really go at it. Now, I only wish she were here to fuss at me, tell me my hair is too wild, my clothes are too radical." She stopped, sucked in a breath, wrapped her arms across her waist. "Seeing these two very mixed-up families has made me realize just how much I miss her and how blessed I was to have her."

Ben saw her expression change, the tears misting over in her eyes. "Have you even given yourself permission to grieve?" he asked gently.

Sara looked at him, surprise clear in her eyes, then whirled as if searching for something to do. "No, I guess I haven't really thought about it. This may sound cruel, but I was…relieved when she finally died.'' She turned to him then, a pleading look in her eyes. ''I just wanted her to find some peace, some control, someplace safe and away from that terrible sickness.''

Ben had her in his arms in two long strides. ''Sara, here I've been whining all day about my problems, about Jason and Patty, and this has obviously upset you, too. I'm sorry.''

''Don't be silly,'' she said, clearly mortified that she'd been about to cry. Sniffing loudly, she tried to laugh. ''I'm a big girl. And I'm okay. It just hits me at the oddest moments.''

''Well, let it hit you,'' he coaxed, lifting her chin to look into her incredible eyes. ''But remember that your mother is safe now, and warm, and she's not suffering anymore. She's with God. I know that sounds pat and condescending, but you have to know she is at peace.''

''I know that. I believe that with all my heart. But I sure do miss her.''

''Do *you* need to go for a walk out by the lake?''

She smiled then, taking what little control he had left completely away. His heart was doing the Sara highstep again.

''No, I'm just fine standing right here.''

''Are you sure you're all right?'' he asked, wanting to make her feel better.

''I'm fine,'' she told him again. ''I've had lots of long walks out by the water, believe me. It does help matters, doesn't it?''

He nodded. "Makes you feel closer to God."

"I guess that's it," she agreed, not bothering to move out of his embrace. "I've never felt so close to God. Being here in Fairweather, with so many good people to lend support, has truly helped me to put my faith back in the proper perspective."

"And what about me?" he asked, his voice betraying him.

"What about you?" She looked up, her eyes wide with wonderment and...maybe just a little doubt.

"Have I helped you to put things into perspective?"

She lifted a hand to his face, her touch warm, her eyes as deep and rich as a forest. "No," she said bluntly. "You've put my whole system into this...this out-of-control tailspin. I don't know about you, Rev."

"I know about you, though," he said, more than pleased that she seemed to be having some of the same symptoms as him. Then before she could bolt out of his arms, he leaned down to kiss her. His hand still held her chin; her hand still rested on his jawline. The chili still bubbled away on the stove, and outside, the winter wind picked up to rattle branches against the many windows.

Sara's sigh filled the tiny kitchen, making Ben smile into her lips, her warm, welcoming lips. He lifted his head then. "Was that a protest or a promise?"

She looked up at him, her face flushed, her hair

mushed, and gave him a crooked little smile. "Depends. Will your chili have the same effect as your kisses?"

"Oh, you mean that slight burning sensation all the way to the tips of your toes?"

"Did I say that?"

"You didn't feel that kiss all the way to your toes?" He feigned confusion. "It's always worked before."

She pulled away then, playfully slapping him on the shoulder. "Either way, I think I'm in for some major heartburn."

Ben let her go to catch his own breath. Well, *he'd* certainly felt that kiss. No amount of chili, spicy or otherwise, could ever compare to the slow burn he felt right now, just looking at her.

Heartburn. Was that what she thought he'd cause her?

She might be right. And he was sure his own heart would suffer in the process.

But he'd sure like to take that risk.

Sara was standing at the windows, apparently trying to distance herself from him as much as she could. She turned then, her eyes lighting up. "Ben, it's snowing."

He came to stand by her. "So it is." Then he looked over at her, saw the delight in her eyes, saw that something else he couldn't put a name to just yet. "First snow. First kiss—if we don't count that little peck I gave you in the church parking lot."

"Who's counting?" she asked, a soft flush of color brightening her cheeks.

"That was just a rehearsal for this," he told her, kissing her again for emphasis. Then he lifted his head so he could gaze down into her eyes. "We could have lots of firsts, you know."

"Like our first chilifest," she said, whirling by him, trying to escape, no doubt.

"Come here," he said as he pulled her back around. "The chili isn't quite ready yet."

"Oh, really? Smells ready to me."

"In another kiss or two, it should be just about right." With that, he tugged her close again. "Let's practice on that heartburn some more."

"So you're telling us that his kisses are right up there with four-alarm chili?" Julianne grinned, then glanced over at Maggie, a twinkle in her eyes. "Who knew old Reverend Ben could set such a fire in a girl's heart?"

Maggie chimed right in, whispering so they wouldn't disturb the babies. "Well, Julianne, you had your chance. But you got stuck with my charming brother Luke instead. Disappointed?"

"Never," Julianne replied, sticking out her tongue. Then she glanced up. "Where's Rachel, anyway? Don't people at city hall get a lunch break?"

"I thought we were talking about Luke," Sara told them as she poured another round of hot tea.

They'd all agreed to meet at the center for a

quick lunch, since time was precious for all of them and they had some last-minute details to go over for both the Harvest Celebration and Betty and Warren's upcoming wedding.

"We were talking about *Ben*," Maggie reminded her, her grin as wide as Julianne's. "Does this mean you might consider staying on after Christmas?"

Before Sara could assure her friend that she had no intentions of remaining in Fairweather, Rachel Talbot came bouncing into the room, clearly out of breath. "Did I miss anything?"

"Just that Ben and Sara shared a kiss—during the first snowstorm the other night," Julianne proudly told her.

"No?" Rachel fell into a chair and grabbed a fresh apple muffin. "Did you two bring on all that fresh snow and then melt it right away again?"

Sara groaned, then sank into her own chair to glare at the other overly interested women sitting around the table. "We didn't bring on anything—"

"Except kisses spicier than four-alarm chili," Maggie reminded her.

"That's not what I said. How'd you two wrangle this out of me, anyway? We were talking about the arts-and-crafts booth, remember?"

"Yes, and I said that you and Ben would be forced to endure four long hours of agony together," Julianne happily reminded her. "And then you said, 'Yeah, and after that kiss the other night—'"

Sara groaned again. Why had she blurted that out? Maybe because kissing Ben had been on her mind since the snowstorm, and maybe because she was worried about being in a tiny booth with him for four hours. "Right." Turning to the confused but highly interested Rachel, she said, "And then they made me tell everything. They threatened to wake all the babies if I didn't spill the whole story."

"Horrid women! And I missed it." Rachel placed her elbows on the table, her gaze cast on Sara. "So you'll just have to tell it all over again."

"No." Sara got to up to go check on Tyler. He'd been a bit fussy all morning. She was pretty sure he might have an ear infection. After checking his diaper, she picked up the baby and brought him over to the corner where all the women were seated.

Rachel automatically pulled up a rocking chair for Sara. "Ben Hunter is a fine man. Aren't I always saying that?"

Maggie cooed at Tyler. "Yes. And we all agree."

Sara looked up from Tyler's cherubic face to find three women smiling smugly at her. With a long sigh, she whispered to the baby, "I think I'm outnumbered here."

"Definitely." Maggie bobbed her head. "If you let him get away—"

Just then, the man of the hour walked into the semidarkened room.

Sara took one look at Ben, then shot a warning glare at her friends. Of course, he looked so handsome standing there in his flannel shirt and jeans. The only time she'd seen him look better was on Sunday mornings when he wore his suit and tie, then donned his robe to deliver the sermon.

He immediately headed to the corner, his gaze moving over each of the amused women. "Ladies, did I interrupt something important?"

"Don't answer that," Sara warned under her breath, all the while rocking Tyler with a serenity she didn't feel.

"You sure did," Julianne retorted, obviously enjoying herself. "Sara was just telling us how much she enjoyed...your...er...chili the other night."

Ben laughed, then cautiously glanced at Sara. "I'm glad she survived my cooking."

"Oh, she survived all right," Maggie told him, her smile completely composed. "Remind me to get that recipe."

Now that they had him flustered, Ben looked even more adorable. Rubbing a hand over his ever-tousled curls, he backed toward the door. "Something tells me I don't want to know what's really going on here." Sending Sara a baffled look, he said, "I just came in to check on Tyler. Is he still fussy?"

"He's a little cranky," Sara told him in her best professional voice, ignoring the giggles and sighs all around. "I'm just getting him back to sleep." Her concern for the baby overriding her friends' teasing looks, she added, "You might want to schedule a doctor's appointment. I think he has an ear infection."

Ben shot across the room then, to touch Tyler's rosy cheek. "No fever, at least. I'll call and make the appointment for this afternoon."

Sara nodded, lifting her gaze to Ben. "And I'll try to keep him comfortable until then. Don't worry."

"I'm not. I know you'll take good care of him."

The room grew silent as they eyed each other. Sara couldn't help but remember how sweet Ben's kisses were. And from the way he was gazing down on her, she felt as if he was remembering, too.

Sara looked up to find her friends enthralled with the whole exchange. Sending them another warning glance, she spoke at last. "I'm going to put him back down in a bit, see if he can rest."

"Then I'll leave you to it." Ben glanced around, and seeing the interested expressions on the faces of the women sitting at the table, blushed, then backed even farther out of the room. "Ladies."

"Bye, Ben."

The chorus of goodbyes reminded Sara of long-ago spend-the-night parties. Had all of her grown-up friends gone completely daft and reverted back to adolescence?

Rachel poked Maggie. "Yeah, right. Came by to check on Tyler."

"More like, to check out Tyler's efficient, lovely

caregiver, I'd say," Julianne whispered, giggling in spite of herself.

"Would you all just drop this," Sara said, half irritated, half elated. "You'll give Ben the wrong idea."

"Or the right one," Maggie said, a warm look passing through her eyes. "I'd be so happy if you two—"

"Well, we aren't," Sara said as she shifted Tyler in her arms. "We're just friends."

"Why?"

The chorus again.

"Because..." She knew there were several very valid reasons why she and Ben couldn't be together, but for some strange reason they all seemed hard to voice right now. "Because I can't stay here, because he's still grieving over Nancy—he can't even bring himself to talk to me about that, even after I poured my heart out to him about losing my mother—and because I'm worried that he's getting too attached to Tyler and that he might get too accustomed to me being around to help him out, then we'll both be gone out of his life and, I don't want to put him through that again."

"Nice speech, but what about you?" Maggie asked gently.

"What about me? I'm fine."

"Are *you* afraid of getting too attached?" Her gaze drifted down to the baby Sara held tightly in her arms.

Sara looked around at the now-silent group of

friends. It had been a long time since she'd felt she could trust anyone, but in spite of their good-natured teasing, she knew she could trust this group with her innermost feelings.

Taking a deep breath, she blurted it all out. "I'm afraid it's too late for that, ladies. I'm already way in over my head. And way too attached to the good reverend and his precious little bundle. There, satisfied?"

To her surprise, none of them laughed or made any teasing remarks. Maggie reached across the table to touch Sara's arm. "We're on your side, you know that."

"We sure are," Rachel said, her expression sincere and warm. "We'll pray that God sends you the answer, whatever decision you make."

Julianne sniffed, causing them all to glance up in alarm. "It's just so…sweet," she said, wiping away a tear. "And…I'm very emotional right now." Then she gave them a shaky smile. "I hear that happens to pregnant women a lot."

Realizing what her friend had just said, Maggie gave a little squeal of delight, then quickly covered her mouth with her hand. "Are you going to have a baby?"

Julianne bobbed her head. "Yes. I'm three months pregnant."

Rachel shot out of her chair, giving Julianne a tight hug. "Oh, Julianne, I'm so happy for you. And I guess that means I can share my news now. I'm going to have a baby, too."

Julianne got up to hug Rachel. "How wonderful! Maybe we'll go into labor together."

Rachel nodded, tears cresting in her eyes. "I'm not quite three months, so let's keep it quiet for a while. But I stay hungry, which is why I can't stop eating these apple muffins."

After hugs all around, tears of joy and many thanks for all their blessings, Sara watched her glowing friends, then held Tyler even tighter. "Two more babies for the nursery. I'm so excited for both of you."

Maggie followed suit. "Me, too. More playmates for Elizabeth Anne."

Sara smiled in spite of the little twinge of regret that nettled its way into her heart. "That's wonderful news, especially for you, Julianne. You thought it couldn't happen."

"Not to me, anyway," Julianne said between a fresh batch of tears. "But it did. So you see, Sara. Nothing is impossible."

"That's right," Maggie reminded her. "We might not get the answers we want, but God will show us the way."

"He certainly has with Morgan and me," Rachel reminded them, her expression full of serenity.

"'Cast all of your cares on Me,'" Sara said, remembering one of her mother's favorite Bible quotes from 1 Peter. "Thank you, all of you, for caring."

"We do," Maggie told her. "And so does God."

After baby talk, wedding talk and final plans for

the weekend festival, the women finished their meeting, then all got back to their jobs, leaving Sara still rocking little Tyler.

And that's how Ben found her a few minutes later. She didn't see him at first, because she had her head bent close to the baby. Listening and watching, he realized she was humming and singing to Tyler, a beautiful lullaby about ponies at the fair.

Ben stood there, taking in the beauty of woman and child, his heart doing its little dance, his soul opening up with a breathtaking clarity. Was there a more beautiful sight in all of God's world?

Sara's burnished curls clung to her cheekbones and her neck, and Tyler's pink little face looked contented, rested, as if the baby knew he was exactly where he should be. So trusting, so precious. Such a perfect picture.

Ben thought of Nancy. Why couldn't he remember her face? Why couldn't he remember her laugh? He'd thought he'd never be able to get her image out of his mind. It troubled him that now Sara's image was slowly replacing that of the woman he had loved and planned to marry. But…maybe that was God's way of telling him he had to let go and move on.

And here was his chance. Here, sitting in this very room, was a woman and a child, and a chance for happiness.

Did he dare tell Sara that he was beginning to

fall in love with her? Did he dare hope that Tyler could truly become his child?

As if sensing the intrusion, Sara looked up then, a little rush of breath leaving her, a surprised expression shining in her eyes. "Ben?"

"Is it safe now?" he said, amazed that he could even find coherent words.

"Very safe." She lifted out of the chair to place the now-sleeping Tyler back in his bed. Her movements were so maternal, so natural. She had a way with children. She also had a way with preachers.

"How's he feeling?" Ben asked on a whisper.

"He seems less restless now. Were you able to get an appointment?"

"Yes. That's why I'm here. Around three."

"I'll have him ready for you."

Then she turned to face Ben. "Is everything all right?"

"Everything is…just fine," he told her.

And yet, that statement wasn't completely honest. Everything wasn't just fine.

Watching her here with Tyler, seeing her in the role of nurturer and surrogate mother, Ben felt as if he'd let go of something he'd been holding on to for a very long time. That something was his heart.

And it both thrilled and terrified him.

Chapter Ten

"You've lost weight. You're way too thin."

Ben's mother stood in the middle of the town square, ignoring the festivities around her while her sharp eyes stayed centered on her son.

Ben looked heavenward, took a deep breath, then grinned down at the petite but tough woman who'd given birth to him.

"Nice to see you, too, Mother."

Alice Hunter waved a hand in dismissal, then reached out to hug him, her light wool cape fluttering around her elbows. "How have you been?"

"I'm doing okay," he told her as he leaned over the booth railing to return his mother's hug, all the while aware of Sara's amused curiosity.

His mother wore a bright green wool fedora over her short, clipped gray hair, making her look more like an Alpine hiker than a college professor.

Ben and Sara were in their assigned booth and the Harvest Celebration was in full swing. Thankfully the weather was holding out and the late fall day had been nice in spite of the cold temperatures. Bundled in lightweight jackets and coats, citizens moved along the town square and mingled in the open shops along the way. Swenson's Bakery was doing a brisk business and Ben already had two sandwiches from Olaf's Deli for Sara and him to munch on later.

In typical fashion, his mother hadn't announced when she'd be arriving. She'd just shown up and walked around greeting people she knew until she found her son.

"Been busy?" Alice asked now, her gaze moving from the attractive offerings inside the craft booth to the woman helping her son hawk them. Before Ben could answer, she extended a tiny, veined hand to Sara. "Hello. I'm Alice Hunter, Ben's mother. My son seems to have lost his tongue."

Ben strangled back a protest, then said, "I fully intended to introduce you two—this is Sara Conroy. She's working in the day-care center until Maggie comes back from maternity leave."

Alice continued to hold Sara's hand. "Well, so this is Sara. Very nice. So glad to meet you, and so glad Maggie finally had that baby." Then she turned to her son. "Now tell me about you—a foster father? When do I get to meet my foster grandchild?"

Ben gave Sara an amused look, then said, "Tyler

is in the church nursery with Sadie. You know Sadie. You met her last time you came for a visit."

"Oh, yes." Alice nodded, then fidgeted with a lovely wedding ring quilt hanging nearby. "Sadie has the best remedy for a cold. It's some kind of spicy tea she got from her Cajun cousin way down in Louisiana. It'll cure what ails you. Do you have any of that available today?"

Sara looked around the booth. "I'm afraid I don't see any Cajun tea, Mrs. Hunter. But we've sold out of a lot of our most sought-after items. I can ask Sadie if she has any stashed away."

"I'll ask her myself," Alice told her, her tone firm and no-nonsense. "When I go to meet little Tyler."

"He's been sick with an ear infection," Ben warned. "Don't juggle him too much."

"I believe I know how to handle a baby, dear," his mother said, a wry smile on her face. "But I promise I'll be gentle."

Dropping her head, she gave Sara a direct look over the rim of her bifocals. "Ben's mentioned you in his letters and phone calls. He told me you were pretty, and I tend to agree."

Sara shot Ben a surprised look, so he shrugged and said, "Well, it's the truth."

Alice watched them with all the harshness that being a college professor dictated, as if she were analyzing them both for some sort of dissertation. Then with a slight smile and a wave of the hand, she turned. "Going to get settled in at the parsonage. Key in the same place?"

"Yes," Ben replied, shrugging silently to Sara. "How long are you planning on staying?"

Alice kept walking away. "Depends," she called over her shoulder. "I'll see you later, son." Then to Sara, "Good to meet you, Miss Conroy."

"You, too, Mrs. Hunter," Sara called, waving to the woman's back. Then she turned to Ben with a long-winded sigh. "Wow, your mother is formidable, to say the least."

Ben ran a hand through his hair, then groaned. "That was her intimidating professor attitude—all five feet, four inches of it. She was scoping you out, sizing you up."

"I could tell. Do you think I'll get a passing grade?"

Ben gave her a mock-professor type look. "Depends," he said in a low, scholarly voice.

Then they both burst out laughing.

"Want some hot chocolate?" he asked Sara, wiping tears of laughter from his eyes while he still chuckled.

"Yes. I need some fortitude after that encounter."

Grinning, he turned and produced a thermos and the deli bag from Olaf's. "Our dinner."

Sara clapped her hands together. "Oh, I'm starved. This booth working sure brings on an appetite."

Ben motioned to the two stools they had set up

in the booth. "Well, let's sit and enjoy this before my mother comes back to dissect our relationship."

Right now, they were between customers, and the handmade quilts surrounding the booth on all sides provided a cozy privacy and a good cover from the crisp late-afternoon wind. Inside the booth, they offered everything from homemade jellies, jams and famous Fairweather maple syrup to decorated wreaths and hand-carved trinkets. Now they were down to a few items.

In the square, the local high school band played a merry polka tune that had everyone tapping their feet, while the food booths continued doing a brisk business by offering everything from fresh-baked apple and pumpkin pies to trout dinners and sausage on a bun.

And all around, the crimson and golden colors of fall, coupled with the remains of the early snow they'd had the other night, merged to form the perfect backdrop of towering maples mixed with birch, pine and aspen trees.

Sara munched the fat sandwich Ben had handed her, then took a long sip of the creamy hot chocolate. "This had been fun," she told him. "I'm tired, but it's the kind of tired that makes you feel good at the end of the day."

Ben held his own cup of cocoa in his hands. "Life's like that around here. Not too fast-paced, but when we get together for a celebration, we always have a good time."

"I never had time for anything like this in the

city," Sara replied, her tone pensive. "It was all work, then home to relieve my mother's sitter."

"It must have been hard, working with those tiny babies every day, then having to turn around and tend to your mother."

Sara looked down at the sandwich she held on her lap. "Yes. Some nights, I'd fall into bed, exhausted, only to be wakened by my mother having a nightmare or wandering around the house, bumping into things. I never really could sleep soundly. I was always worried she'd fall and hurt herself."

"I can't imagine seeing my mother like that," Ben said, his expression full of understanding. "As you just witnessed, she's a character, sort of a human dynamo. It would be hard to watch, hard to accept her as anything but the independent, stubborn mother I love."

"I guess it depends on the person, too," Sara told him. "My mother never was very strong, and she seemed to go downhill after my father died."

She watched as Ben sat silent for a minute, hoping he'd open up to her in the same way she'd shared things with him. Since their time together out at her cottage on the lake, he'd seemed quieter, maybe a little distant. Or maybe she was imagining things. Maybe she'd even imagined the wonder of their shared kisses. She'd certainly tried to put all the strange new feelings bubbling up inside her out of her mind.

But here she sat, closer than ever to the man who'd changed her whole perspective, her whole outlook on life, in a matter of a few weeks. Yet that man couldn't seem to trust her with the secret hurts from his own past. And she couldn't seem to bring herself to confess to him that she already knew everything she needed to know about him. She just wished Ben could let someone share his burdens, the way he took on those of everyone else.

"Why are you staring at me?" Ben asked now, wiping a hand across his chin. "Do I have some of Olaf's famous hot mustard sauce on my face?"

Sara laughed, then shook her head. "I'm sorry. I guess seeing your mother has just made me wonder about you—you know, you as a little boy, in high school, those wild college days—"

"Hey, I attended seminary—that didn't get any wilder than a late night studying the gospels, trust me."

He was using another diversion technique, but Sara pressed on. "So...tell me about Ben Hunter anyway. Or do I have to ask your mother?"

He looked genuinely concerned then. Taking a napkin out of the sandwich bag, he wiped his hands then gave her his full attention. "Do not ask my mother anything. She'd tell you way more than you ever wanted to know."

"Why don't *you* tell me?" Sara asked, her tone completely serious.

"Why is it so important that you know?"

"Because...we're friends. And you know everything about me."

That silence again. Then Ben glanced up at her,

his eyes holding hers. She could almost see the questions forming on his forehead. Could he trust her? Could he make her understand that he liked her, cared about her, enjoyed her company, but he was still hung up on the woman he'd lost, the one woman he'd planned a life with?

She waited, not making it easy for him, since he'd turned her life inside out. Sara needed to know, needed to hear the words from him.

Ben reached a hand out to her. "There's a lot you don't know," he said, his voice low and serious. "And maybe it is time I told you some things about my past."

Sara took his hand, held it in hers, remembering his kisses, remembering what a good and decent man he was. "I want to know, Ben."

But it wasn't to be. In the next instant, she looked up to find Richard and Mary Erickson standing at their booth, their frowning faces indicating that they did not approve of their minister holding hands with a woman in public.

"Mr. Erickson," Ben said, standing to extend his hand to the other man. "How are you, sir?"

"How do you think?" Richard Erickson replied, barely acknowledging the handshake. "After everything you told us during our last meeting, you should know we're no better off than we were before you went to New Hope."

Sara saw the disappointment come over Ben's face. He'd told her about that last meeting with the Ericksons. After he'd explained to Jason's parents that there was a good possibility that Jason and Patty had run away together, based on the information Reverend Brooks and Patty's parents had given him, the Ericksons had once again turned hostile, blaming Ben for bringing Jason and Patty together in the first place.

"I guess you haven't found out anything more," Ben said, his gaze falling on Mary Erickson. "Mrs. Erickson, I wish there was something I could say—"

"I've got private detectives and the police looking into the matter," Richard retorted, interrupting with a hand in the air. "I suggest you stay out of it from now on."

"You know I can't do that," Ben told the stubborn man. "I have a responsibility to Jason."

"You *are* responsible for all of this," Richard said, his eyes blazing with anger. "You've done quite enough already."

Mary looked as if she were about to cry. "Reverend, I do appreciate your going to New Hope. At least now we have a little more information. And I can rest a little better, thinking maybe Jason's not alone out there."

"No, he's never alone," Ben told her. "God is watching over him and I pray that God will lead him home again."

Richard snorted, then shook a finger at Ben. "My son is out there with some girl we know nothing about, doing things we surely don't approve, and all you can say is that you pray God will lead him home. You'd better do more than that, Reverend. You'd better pray that I don't have you kicked out of the church.''

Sara stood up then, anger clouding her better judgment. "Excuse me, but don't you think you're being a little too harsh on Ben? He's done everything in his power to help find Jason and I believe he did a good job in counseling your son before he ran away.''

Richard turned on her then. "And just who do you think you are, telling me all of this? You weren't even here when this man put all these notions into my son's head.''

"No, I wasn't here," Sara replied, her voice calm in spite of her fast beating pulse. "But I've been here long enough to see that Ben Hunter is a good minister and that he cares about children. He would never purposely do anything to bring Jason to destruction.''

"It's mighty noble of you to stand up for him," Richard told her, "since it's obvious you two are carrying on just as much as my son and this—this girl he took up with." He jabbed a finger at Ben. "And him trying to raise a baby, too. All he's done is pass that child around from church member to church member. That's not the kind of role model I want for my son—not him, and certainly not you, either, since you seem to be just as liberal-minded as him.''

"That's enough," Ben said, clearly frustrated. Running a hand through his hair, he let out a long breath. "Mr. Erickson, Sara Conroy and I are just good friends. She helps me out with Tyler and she works in the day-care center. I won't allow you to slander her, no matter what your opinion of me may be."

"He's absolutely right," came a tightly controlled voice from behind them. "My son does not need the likes of you telling him how he should be conducting his private life."

The Ericksons whirled to find Alice Hunter standing there looking for all the world like a mother lioness protecting one of her cubs.

"Hello, Mary," she said sweetly, her eyes flashing at Richard. "I'm so sorry about Jason. You know, when Ben was that age, he went through a rather bad period. Did not listen to me, and refused to follow my authority. I sent him to our minister and I haven't regretted doing it, not once. I'm praying that your Jason will come to his senses and return safely to you, but in the meantime I won't have you putting all the blame on my son."

Richard turned to face her, his face red with rage. "*Your* son is trying to raise some foundling baby and he's carrying on in public with a woman. Doesn't that sound out of sync with being a man of God?"

"Sounds right in sync to me," Alice said on a huff. "He's taken in a child that needed help, and he's found a lovely woman to spend time with, all the while maintaining his church responsibilities and dealing with the likes of you. I'd say he's doing a pretty good job, too."

"Mother, I don't need you running interference for me," Ben said, a hand up to halt Alice.

Sara noticed that Alice seemed ready to continue her lecture. In spite of the uncomfortable scene in front of her, she had to smile. A mother's love was an awesome thing.

"You're right, son, you don't," Alice told him. Then turning to Mary, she asked, "Could we go have a good hot cup of tea, dear?"

Looking shocked, Mary glanced at her husband. "I...I don't know."

"You look as if you could use a friend," Alice said, taking the woman by the arm. "Richard, Mary is going with me for a while. You don't mind, do you?"

Richard Erickson looked as if he'd been hit by a truck. "I'm going home," he said to everyone in general. "Mary, you know where to find me."

With that, he turned and marched away, scattering fallen leaves all around his feet as he hurried off.

"I think the festival is just about over," Alice said. "Ben, why don't you close up and take Sara and Tyler home?"

"Thanks, Mother," Ben said grudgingly. As he watched his mother guiding the dazed and confused Mary Erickson off, he let out another frustrated sigh. "Great—I have to have two women fighting my battles for me now."

"We did it because we believe in you," Sara told him. "And because you're caught in a very awkward position, being the minister. You couldn't very well deck the man."

He shook his head. "No, that would be just the ticket he needs to get rid of me for good."

"Okay, then stop beating yourself up. You handled the situation well enough, and being a macho man wouldn't make things any better." Touching a hand to his arm, she added, "You certainly came to my rescue fast enough."

Ben lifted his head, his gaze meeting hers. "I won't let him think anything bad about you."

"Oh, right. But it's okay for him to think the worst of you."

"He might be right there."

Her hand still on his arm, Sara shook her head. "No, Ben. He's upset, bitter, grasping for somewhere to lay the blame, but I think in his heart, Richard Erickson is so full of guilt, that he feels it necessary to hide behind blaming you. But you are not to blame here."

Ben put his hand over hers, then lifted her hand to his mouth so he could kiss it briefly. "I appreciate the vote of confidence. But maybe...maybe both Mr. Erickson and I are to blame here. Neither of us saw the warning signs, neither of us knew Jason had a girlfriend. Maybe we both blew it."

"It's going to work out," Sara told him, trying to reassure him. "You've certainly taught me to believe that no matter what, God has a plan for all of us."

"Do *you* really believe in *me?*" Ben asked her then, his heart in his blue eyes.

"I do." She just wished *he* believed in her enough to trust her, and to let her help him get over his own grief. He'd come so close to telling her, to sharing all of his burdens with her, but now she didn't want to press him. Not after that terrible scene with Jason's father.

"Let's go home," Ben told her, his whole attitude changing from lighthearted to disheartened right before her eyes.

Silently they cleaned up their booth, then secured the rest of their wares for the owners to claim later.

Just as they were about to leave, Ben caught Sara by the sleeve of her sweater. "Hey, I almost forgot."

She turned in surprise to find him holding a small white box. "What's this?"

"I—I bought it for you, before the mad rush. Actually, I special-ordered it about a week ago."

Touched and curious, Sara took the box. "Can I open it?"

He managed a lopsided smile. "Sure."

She lifted the lid off, then let out a gasp of delight. A dainty necklace lay nestled in the fluffy cotton of the box. Holding it up, Sara surveyed the necklace in the glow of the sunset. It looked like carved wood—tiny colorful beads that formed a chain, with a beautiful wooden cross hanging at its center. In the center of the cross was a small, beautiful dark-veined stone that curved inward in the middle.

"One of our Native American church members carved and designed this by hand," Ben explained. "The stone comes from the bluffs overlooking the Mississippi River—granite and limestone, I think. It's sunken in like that because it's a worry stone." He took her thumb and placed it in the center of the stone, then pressed her hand underneath to hold the cross. "See, you can rub it while you're worrying over something, or praying about something."

Amazed that her thumb fit perfectly over the stone, Sara held it, rubbing the polished veins. It felt warm and comforting against her skin. "It's beautiful, Ben," she told him, the lump in her throat making it hard to speak.

"I thought you could wear it to remember that you're not alone."

"I have my rock," she said, touching on the smooth stone. "Thank you."

"You're welcome." He leaned close to steal a quick kiss. "You do have a rock, you know. God has always been right there with you."

Sara nodded, then placed the long beaded chain around her neck. It fit perfectly against her skin. She understood what Ben was saying. Since coming here, she'd found God in everything, from the soothing blue waters of Lake Baylor to the enchanting, calming blue of Ben Hunter's eyes.

She'd found her rock all right, in God, and in the man who'd just given her this beautiful cross necklace.

The man she was falling in love with.

She . . . hadn't wanted to check in what, and it
all was what just given for this beautiful new
necklace.

For right she was filling it just with.

Chapter Eleven

"Son, I've fallen in love with Carl Winslow and
we're getting married next spring."

Alice Hunter took another sip of her breakfast
coffee, then went about buttering her toast with
dainty efficiency while Ben tried not to choke on
his wheat cereal.

"Reverend Carl Winslow?" he squeaked, knowing it was a redundant question.

Alice fussed with Tyler. The baby had just finished a big breakfast bottle and was now content
to gurgle and kick in his sturdy carrier while the
adults finished up.

"Do you know another Carl Winslow?"

"No, Mother. Of course not." He waved a hand,
then caught his breath. "This…this is a surprise."

"Yes, it was to me, too," Alice said, her gaze
turning dreamy. "But you know how that goes,

son. One day you're going along, perfectly content with your little life, then boom, something happens to make you see things in a completely new light.''

Ben glanced over at his mother, making sure she wasn't sleepwalking. Yes, he certainly could relate to that kind of boom. He'd felt the same way since Sara Conroy had shown up in his own life.

Right now, however, he didn't have time to dwell on how much Sara had affected his life. Now he really needed to understand the news his mother had just dropped on him. ''I guess so, since you've known Carl Winslow for about twenty years now, and since you purposely sent me to him that summer so long ago for guidance. You two have always been friends, Mother. Remember? Just friends?'' Eyeing her sharply, he said, ''Did you get hit on the head?''

''No, nothing like that.'' Alice actually giggled, then cooed to Tyler. ''More like I got hit in the heart.''

Ben felt aggravated that his own mother had found someone to share her life with, while it looked like he'd remain a bachelor the rest of his days. Squinting to hide the very real resentment he felt, he pushed away his jealousy and gave his mother what he hoped was an encouraging smile. ''Mother, you're going to have to catch me up on things.''

''There's not much to catch up,'' Alice replied. Dusting toast crumbs off her hands, she leaned forward. ''Carl and I just suddenly realized we'd both been alone long enough. I lost your father a long time ago, but it took me many years to let him go. And Carl lost his sweet Janey ten years ago. We were both so busy trying to ignore our grief, that we forgot to celebrate life.'' She shrugged, an eloquent, dainty lifting of her tiny shoulders. ''And now...well, we're both headed toward retirement and I guess the loneliness finally got the best of us.''

''So you're marrying Carl Winslow for companionship?''

''No, I'm marrying him because he's a fine, good man and I love him. And I hope you'll approve and give us your blessings.''

Ben looked up then to find his mother watching him, her expression hopeful. Alice Hunter had never asked for anyone's approval; she'd just lived her life in a way that always warranted instant approval. Her value system was as intact as her grading system—and both tough to argue with. Now it humbled Ben to see that his strong, independent mother was asking, hoping for his support.

And here he sat, feeling sorry for himself instead of rejoicing because his mother had at last found someone to grow old with, someone to love and share her wonderful, incredible life with. Mentally kicking himself for being so selfish, Ben immediately changed his attitude. He wouldn't begrudge his hardworking mother any happiness. She deserved so much more; Alice Hunter relished life, loved the Lord and understood things about people that most never took the time to see. Ben wanted to share in her joy, not crush it with harsh words or his own bitterness.

He got up to come around the breakfast table. "Of course I approve, Mother," he said as he leaned down to give her a hug. "I love Carl Winslow. He's been like a father to me, and we both know he saved me from myself long ago. If you two can find some happiness together, who am I to judge? I can't think of a better person for you to spend your golden years with."

Alice hugged him so tightly, she cut off his breath, but Ben didn't complain. It felt good to be hugged.

"They will be golden now," she told him. "I just wanted you to understand."

"I do. It's a surprise, though. You never even mentioned that you two were…close."

"It took me a while to admit my feelings," Alice said. Then she asked, "Speaking of which…how do you feel about Sara Conroy?"

Ben sank back down, then gave Tyler a bewildered look. Alice Hunter didn't carry on a conversation in the normal way. No, his mother had to keep throwing him for a loop, sending him surprise after surprise by bluntly changing the subject with the same economic speed in which she granted grades on term papers. Never a dull moment, and he wouldn't have it any other way. Only, right now, he wished he could have it another way. He didn't know how to answer her question, and he surely didn't enjoy the all-seeing glare of her intense, questioning eyes.

"Don't get all pensive on me," Alice said, her sharp gaze centered on her son. "Tell me."

Ben leaned back in his chair, then crossed his arms over his chest. "Would you believe we're just friends?"

"No."

"Would you believe me if I told you I don't know how I feel about Sara?"

"No."

"Okay. I give up. Why don't *you* tell *me* how I feel about Sara?"

Alice bobbed her head, then adjusted her reading glasses. "Okay. I think you've fallen in love with her, but you've got so much else to deal with right now, you don't have time to pursue her properly. You don't have time to court her, woo her, show her how much you've come to appreciate her. You're worried about Jason Erickson, about raising little Tyler, about maintaining some sort of control over your flock, and you probably think that Sara just considers you a friend. You also probably are feeling a little guilty because you've refused to so much as look at another woman since Nancy's death. And because of that, you can't bring yourself to even tell that nice girl that you care about her."

Ben scratched his head, then stared across the table at his smug mother. "Are you by any chance a college professor, 'cause you sure are smart."

"Just logic and deduction, son," Alice said on a

soft voice. "And a mother's eyes. I saw the way you looked at her during the Harvest Celebration, and the other morning in church. Your father always had a special look, just for me. I saw that same kind of look in your eyes when you glanced at Sara."

"You and half the town," Ben said on a huff. "I'm surprised Emma hasn't rented a billboard proclaiming that I'm in love with Sara Conroy."

"Are you?"

"Would you believe me if I denied it?"

"No. But I do believe that, like your mother, you're so busy ignoring your grief over Nancy you won't allow yourself to even consider loving another woman." Taking his hand in hers, Alice looked into her son's eyes. "Don't wait too long, Ben. Life is a gift, a gift that should be shared with someone special. I think Sara is special to you, but you're afraid to admit it."

Ben got up to empty the soggy remains of his cereal. "You're right. She is special. She's different. Funny, loving, very outspoken—just like someone else I happen to love." He pointed a finger at his mother then. "I think I'm falling in love with Sara, but she doesn't know. At least *I* haven't told her."

"And why not?"

Ben stood there staring out the window, watching as the wind blew maple leaves across his backyard. "I don't think she's ready for anything fur-

ther. She just came out of a bad relationship. Her
fiancé dumped her and moved away.''

''That is sad, but you can change all of that. You
two look so lovely together, and she seems to genuinely care about baby Tyler.''

At the mention of his name, the baby squealed
in delight and kicked his booties high.

''She does love Tyler,'' Ben agreed, turning to
play with the woven tie on Tyler's colorful sweater
suit. ''I just don't know how she really feels about
me. When we're together, everything seems so
right, but when I try to take things to a new level,
she backs away.''

''She's scared. You're both scared,'' Alice said,
coming to stand by him. ''I know it was tough
when you lost Nancy, but maybe this is a second
chance for you. After all this time, maybe you've
been hit in the heart, too, son.''

Ben turned and hugged his mother close again.
''You're right about that. And it hurts.''

Alice patted her son on the cheek with maternal
force. ''It's not supposed to hurt, Ben. It's supposed
to feel good, wonderful, right. And you'll never
experience any of those things if you don't tell that
woman how you feel about her.''

''How do you feel about all of this?''

Ben looked down at the man sitting in his office,
then shrugged underneath the heavy black material
of his robe. He was about to marry Betty Anderson
and Warren Sinclair, and he'd gone out to the Fair-

weather Retirement Center to pick up Reverend Olsen for the occasion. On the ride back into town, Ben had told his friend about his mother's upcoming wedding plans, as well as all of his many other concerns right now. It had felt good to be able to share his burdens with someone who wouldn't judge him or condemn him. Reverend Olsen always just listened and offered gentle advice. Which was exactly what Ben needed right now.

Now the two of them were about to enter the church for the current nuptials and Ben had never felt so miserable in his life.

"I'm happy for my mother and Reverend Winslow," he said in an honest voice, "but...I guess I just worry about her. She's been on her own for so long now."

"Your mother is a smart, self-assured woman," Reverend Olsen told him in his leathery old voice. "She knows what she's doing, son."

"Yes, she's always known what she's about," Ben replied. "She's a scholar, but she relies on *this* book first and always." He picked up his Bible then and offered a hand to the older man. "I wish I could say the same for her son, though. I rely on my Bible, but I'm not sure what I'm all about."

Reverend Olsen started to stand, his bent form slow in raising from the chair. But his crystal-blue eyes were as sharp as ever. "Troubles?"

Ben shook his head. "Just self-pity, I'm afraid. It seems everyone around me is getting married.

And here I stand, still alone. Maybe that's God's plan for me, after all.''

The older man gave him a knowing smile. ''The good Lord can only guide you so far, son. It's up to you to go out and look for a helpmate.''

Ben had to laugh at that. ''I guess I can't expect someone to just show up on my doorstep and say, 'Here I am,' now can I?''

Reverend Olsen shuffled toward the door. ''You mean, no one like that has come along lately?''

Ben didn't miss the teasing note in the old man's words. Letting go of an edgy sigh, he held the door. ''Have you been talking to Betty and Emma?''

A deep chuckle filled the quiet room. ''Well, they do come by and visit me from time to time, and we do tend to catch up on the news. You've been very busy lately.''

''You mean because of Tyler?''

''Yes, with a baby to take care of and...from what I hear, a very nice young lady to court.''

''Court? That's the exact word my mother used. Sara and I are not courting.''

''Then what are you two doing?''

''We're friends. Just good friends.''

The reverend turned as they approached the side doors to the sanctuary, where even now the guests were arriving and soft music played in honor of the happy couple. ''The best marriages start out as just friendship, Ben.''

Ben stopped and looked down at his wise mentor. ''You do have a point.''

"Unlike most of my sermons, huh?"

"You preached some of the best sermons I've ever heard."

"And you are a good preacher yourself," Reverend Olsen told him, reaching up like a father to straighten his young charge's white stole. "You're just lonely. That's your problem, son."

"So everybody tells me," Ben replied. "Oh, well, now is not the time to bemoan my forlorn love life. We've got a wedding to attend."

"So we do." Reverend Olsen lifted a shaking, gnarled hand. "See you at the reception."

Ben gave Reverend Olsen a quick wave, then stepped into the little annex where Warren Sinclair and his best man, his son-in-law, Kenny, were waiting. Reverend Olsen's words rang in Ben's head as he wished Warren well and assured him the wedding would go off without a hitch.

The best marriages start out just as friendship, Ben.

The same thing had apparently happened to his mother. She and Carl had started out as friends and now they were in love. It made Ben pause to think about his feelings for Sara.

Could that be the answer he'd been seeking so hard? Could friendship make a good match? His friendship with Sara was strong and complete, no doubt there. And while he could admit to himself that he loved her, he knew she might not be able to return that love. But could she settle for being his wife—out of friendship, for companionship? And for Tyler's sake?

The matter was certainly worth pursuing. And the idea perked him up considerably. Grinning, he slapped Warren on the back. "Don't look so anxious. Your bride's going to show up."

Kenny teased his father-in-law good-naturedly. "Yep, I've never seen such a big, strapping man look so much like a whipped puppy."

Warren let out a shaky breath, then rubbed his chin. "I feel like a pup—a lovesick pup." Then he smiled, the warmth of that smile transcending any physical discomfort. "But it's worth every minute of suffering through this, boys. Take it from me, finding the right woman is worth the agony."

Ben felt a familiar wrench of pain in his own midsection. He wanted to know that certain agony. He wanted a wife of his own. And now he thought he might have just found a way for that to happen—if he could also find a way to get Sara to agree to marry him.

"The wedding was beautiful," Sara told Ben much later as they stood with the other guests in the fellowship hall next to the old church.

The sanctuary had been decorated in all the colors of fall. Since Betty Anderson was the outdoors type and enjoyed fishing and hunting as much as her groom, they'd agreed they wanted as much of the outdoors inside on their wedding day as possible. The effect, while different from any wedding theme Sara had seen, had turned out quite lovely.

They'd used salmon-colored rose trees decorated with twinkling lights on each side of the altar, and the centerpiece had been a large cornucopia— Emma's idea of symbolism for their overflowing love and many blessings—filled to the brim with golden, burgundy and russet mums and lots of fresh greenery. The whole church had smelled as fresh as the great Minnesota woods surrounding Betty's beloved home out on Baylor Lake.

"Betty sure made a striking bride," Ben said now, his gaze following the happy couple as they laughed and talked to Reverend Olson.

"She sure did." Sara couldn't help but feel a tug of regret and envy. She wanted to tell him he'd made a striking minister, in his dark robe with his hair glistening in the candlelight. But that would have been too sappy and intimate. Best to stick to safe subjects, such as the happy bride and groom.

Betty looked so radiant in her cream-colored wool suit and the triple strand of pearls and matching earrings Warren had given her, and the groom, in his dark wool suit, his graying hair clipped close to his head, didn't look half-bad either. They made a wonderful couple.

Sara longed for the day she would walk down the aisle. She was beginning to think it would never happen. Then she looked up to find Ben watching her, and blushed down to her toes.

"What's the matter?" she asked, noticing the

bright gleam in his eyes. "You look as if you have a secret."

"Maybe I do," he said, his grin taking her breath away. "You know, I was in a rotten mood before the wedding. These past few weeks since my mother informed me she was getting married, all this worry about Jason, Tyler being up most nights with that tenacious ear infection, everything—it has all taken its toll. I whined to Reverend Olsen and as usual he put it all in perspective for me."

"So now you have a goofy grin on your face and an interesting gleam in your eyes. Whatever did that man say to you?"

Ben shook his head. "Ah, now, I can't reveal my private conversations with my mentor, can I?"

"Why not?"

"I don't want to give it away just yet."

Sara lifted her head to stare over at him. "Well, all right, then. I won't make you bare your soul. But whatever you two discussed, it's had a definite effect on you. You look positively giddy."

"Weddings do that to me," Ben told her, a hand on her arm. "Let's go sample that black forest cake on the groom's table."

"But we've already sampled the white chocolate wedding cake. You had two russet candy roses and a sugar-coated maple leaf on the side, remember?"

"Yes, and they were incredibly delicious. Mrs. Swenson hasn't lost her touch with icing."

Sara had to laugh. "Good thing you still play basketball on a weekly basis."

He patted his stomach. "I try to stay in shape, in spite of all the good cooks around me."

"And you being single and all, they just can't help but spoil you. I admire women who can cook, though. I'm afraid the man I marry will either have to cook for himself or starve."

Her smile died on her lips as her eyes met his. The look he gave her had nothing to do with food. And neither did his next words, spoken in that deep gravelly voice.

"The man you marry will be fortunate, regardless of how you cook his food."

Sara swallowed, suddenly feeling too warm in her light green wool dress. Glancing around the crowded room to hide her turmoil, she mustered a nervous chuckle. "You think so?"

Ben gently nudged her chin around with one finger, forcing her to look at him. "I'm sure of it. Food is easy to come by. Finding a soul mate is what's hard in life."

Sara tore her gaze away from Ben to search out Betty and Warren. "*They* sure look happy, don't they?"

"Yes. God led them straight to each other."

She ventured another glance at him. There it was. That same knowing look—that secretive, almost smug look. What did he have in mind? Her heart hammered a message to her notion-filled head. Maybe Reverend Ben Hunter had some ideas about them—about her and him and this whole marriage thing. No, that would be crazy. That would be impossible. Yet the look on his face seemed so hope-ful, and the way he kept staring at her. There was something different about Ben today, something more intimate and personal.

Quickly Sara again went over the list of reasons against such a match. She wasn't preacher's wife material, she couldn't even cook—and Ben wasn't over his first love. He couldn't even bring himself to talk about that with her. No, she was reading him all wrong. He was just in a silly, romantic mood because of the wedding.

That had to be it.

And yet her heart soared with the hope that maybe Ben was beginning to have real feelings for her. That they might have a chance, after all. In spite of all the obstacles she saw in their way, Sara couldn't help but hope.

Maybe Ben Hunter had fallen in love with her.

Chapter Twelve

Ben stood by the windows of Betty and Warren's big, rambling house, looking out over the snow-covered hills that led down to Baylor Lake. A few more weeks and they'd be able to ice-skate down there. Soon, Betty would have Warren out ice-fishing, and he'd heard them talking at the dinner table about getting in some skiing now that the powdery snow was settling in for the winter.

Everyone had a life, but the minister of the church.

No, that really wasn't fair to Tyler. The baby had become Ben's life, and while Ben in no way resented having the child to care for, he only wished he had someone to share his newfound joy with. He loved little Tyler, loved watching the baby grow and change almost on a daily basis. Tyler had just had his three-month checkup and, in spite of the bout with ear infections, he seemed to be thriving. Ben had realized during that checkup that he didn't even know the baby's birthday.

Maybe that was why he felt in such a state of limbo, as if his life had suddenly gone still and he didn't know where to go from here. That, and trying to make two very important changes in his life—he wanted to adopt Tyler and he wanted to marry Sara. Yet here he stood, as frozen in place as the lake waters surrounding the dock just below the trees.

Ben closed his eyes and relived the last few weeks since he'd gotten the notion in his head to ask Sara to marry him. Never one to rush into a situation, he'd thought his plan through a thousand times, and a thousand times more he'd decided it was too risky, too foolish to even hope that Sara would agree to marry him based on friendship alone.

He now knew he was in love with her, completely, without a doubt. He'd prayed about it, asked God to give him the courage to approach her about this marriage, asked God to help him get over her if she refused his offer and left Fairweather, but he'd gotten no answers, no signs as to what he should do next.

Sara remained a constant in his life, a friend he knew he could count on, but she hadn't tried to take things beyond that. She'd helped with Tyler, sitting with the baby during the roughest times, her patience and skills leaving Ben wondering how he would have ever managed without her. Still, she'd given him no signs of taking their relationship beyond friendship.

And he'd gotten no signs about Jason, either. The boy hadn't called in weeks, and Richard Erickson's private detectives hadn't found a trace of his son or Patty Martin. Ben was so worried about his young friend. Christmas was coming, and the thought of Jason being away from his family and friends during this most holy of seasons nearly broke Ben's heart.

Then there was the matter of little Tyler. Ben had officially applied to adopt the little boy, but the red tape of not knowing his parentage was stalling the whole process. At least he could still be a foster father to Tyler, until the state decided what to do about the child.

Ben said another prayer, hoping his worst fear wouldn't come true. What if someone else adopted Tyler? What if the state refused Ben's petition, because he was single? Or what if the real parents came forward and contested the adoption? So many questions, so much to struggle with, when he should be standing solid in his faith. Ben just didn't know where to turn anymore.

The scent of Sara's soap-clean floral perfume drifted to Ben's nostrils and he turned to find her standing there beside him with a large mug of hot chocolate. "Betty sent this. She noticed you'd left the meeting, and suggested I come and find you before the fur starts flying."

He took the warm mug, then shrugged, his face twisting in reference to the need to soothe ever-battling committee members. "I'm sorry. I needed to stretch my legs. I love the Christmas season, but it's a busy time for the church. I wanted to find a quiet moment and get in the proper state of mind. I won't let my dark mood put a damper on our Christmas bazaar and all the holiday traditions my church holds so dear."

Sara wrapped her fingers around her own mug of hot chocolate. "I thought you seemed a little down. Anything I can do to help?"

If only she knew, Ben thought, his smile self-deprecating. "Will you stay through the holidays?"

He enjoyed the way she blushed and started fidgeting with her unruly curls. "I hope to."

Ben saw that hope in her green eyes. In moments such as these, he could almost believe Sara might have feelings for him, too. But he couldn't be sure.

They'd spent Thanksgiving together, along with Maggie and Frank and most of their relatives. Ben's mother and Reverend Winslow had come for the event, too. They hoped to be back for Christmas, since it was easier on Ben to keep little Tyler in his own home, and as Alice had told him, "We're free to travel when the mood hits us."

"Are you still concerned about your mother?" Sara asked him now, bringing his thoughts back full circle.

"No." He took a sip of the rich cocoa, then shook his head. "They are so happy, and they're good for each other. As I've told you, Reverend Winslow was like a father to me."

Sara patted him on the arm. "And now he can be your father in every sense of the word."

"Yes. I've been blessed with a wonderful, if not a bit eccentric, mother, and now I'll have someone else I also hold dear to lean on, turn to when I'm in doubt."

"Do you still have doubts?" She set her empty mug on a nearby Victorian table. "About God, I mean."

Ben couldn't resist taking her hand in his. "Never about God, but sometimes about myself. I want to keep Tyler with me, and I'm working toward that, but it doesn't look so good." He dropped his hand away, then looked out toward the lake waters. "You tried to warn me not to get too attached. But I'm afraid it's too late. I think it was too late the moment I heard Tyler crying in the back of the church."

Needing to see her reaction, he ventured further, his gaze sweeping over her face. "I'm attached to Tyler *and* to the woman who's taken care of him since the very first day. I don't know what I'm going to do when both of you are gone."

He saw the confusion, the hesitation in her expression. "You don't know yet if you'll lose Tyler. Where's that faith you're always telling me I should have?"

He gave her a wry smile. "I have the faith, but I can't make the system work for me if there's a better home out there for Tyler. That wouldn't be fair to him."

"You'd let him go, for his own sake." At his slow nod, she added on a tremor, "Ben, there is no greater love than that. Maybe that's why someone left him with you in the first place, because they loved him enough to give him a better home, a better life."

"I just wish I knew who that someone was, so I could convince them that I'll always take care of the gift they bestowed on me."

"You love him."

"I do love that little boy," he told her, the catch in his throat making it hard to speak. "And yes, I'd have to let him go if I thought he'd be better off somewhere else, with a loving, *complete* family."

She pushed at a wayward curl. "It makes me so angry—the way the authorities think you might not be suitable to raise Tyler. You're a minister. Doesn't that count for something?"

"In the eyes of the law, that's just a title. They have to weigh everything."

"Well, it stinks."

He laughed then at her self-righteous indignation, even while his heart was slowly melting into little puddles of longing. "I'll miss you, Sara."

The look she gave him was full of longing, too. And yet she held back, hesitant, her whole expression filled with a questioning doubt. "St. Paul isn't that far," she said. "You can come to visit me in the big city."

"Sure." Ben tilted his head, watching her as she took their mugs. "You know what I think?"

"What?"

"I think I might not ever see you again, once you leave Fairweather."

"What makes you think that?"

He had to find out the truth, had to see if he could bring himself to suggest that she stay. "You seem to have this shield up around you. Sara, you've been a good friend to me, but I know that's all you can ever be. I just wish…I wish we could have gotten closer."

"Ben, we are close," she told him, her eyes glistening. "But I never gave you any false promises. I tried to be honest with you, tried to make you see that all I can offer is friendship. You will always have that."

"It's a start," he said, more to himself than to her.

Why wouldn't she take things any further with him? Hadn't he shown her that he could be trusted? He had a sneaking suspicion she didn't want to get any closer to him because he was a minister. Maybe Sara wasn't willing to turn her life over to God in the same way Ben had. Maybe she didn't want to get involved with someone who always had to put others first—sometimes before his own family.

But he couldn't believe that in his heart. He'd seen Sara with the children at the center. She was more than willing to put others first. She did so every day. And she'd certainly put her mother first, sacrificing both her career and personal life to help a loved one. Sara was capable of being a minister's wife—unless she didn't think so herself.

Ben watched as she headed back into the den where several church members were going over the Advent schedule. Sara had only come to this meeting as a favor to Betty, to help out with serving the refreshments and entertaining any children who'd tagged along—again an example of her willingness to be helpful.

As Ben stood there, his mind raced with the possibilities of being with Sara. If she was afraid of not measuring up, that would explain her deliberate efforts to hold him at arm's length. Maybe he could convince her otherwise. And maybe he could convince her that starting a marriage as friends wouldn't be such a bad thing.

But first he had to find some quiet time to talk to her about his idea, his hope that they might get married.

It did seem that they only managed to get together at church functions or at work. Too many distractions. That brought another idea to mind. They'd never really had a real date. Both his mother, Alice and his friend, Reverend Olsen, had suggested Ben needed to "court" Sara. Maybe he should try doing just that, before she did head back to St. Paul. If he gave her the option of marrying him, it might help solve her future, too. She only wanted friendship, but marriage would bring both of them companionship, too. It was worth a shot.

Feeling immensely better, Ben lifted up a prayer of thanks then strolled back into the den, where a lively bickering session over how to conduct the Christmas Eve services was taking place.

"Here's our leader," Betty said to the lady who'd just raised her voice to be heard, her tone just below a huff. "Let's let Ben decide which music we should use."

"'Joy to the World,'" Ben said immediately, bringing all the fussing to a halt. "'Joy to the world, the Lord is come. Let earth receive her King.'"

Betty shot him a grateful grin. "Certainly one of my favorites. Any other suggestions?"

"How about 'Peace on Earth'?" Ben gave the group a lopsided smile. "And especially, peace between committee members."

Everyone laughed then, breaking the tension between the several domineering, well-meaning church members who always wanted to control everything.

Ben leaned his hands on the back of a floral armchair. "We have many beautiful songs that we traditionally sing on Christmas Eve. So let's get serious about this. While we want the music for this special service to be beautiful, let's remember what's really important. We are celebrating the birth of the Savior, Jesus Christ. The songs don't matter so much as the singers. We need to rejoice and lift our voices high, and we need to remember why we're singing in the first place.''

Several hearty amens followed Ben's minisermon. Those who'd been arguing the loudest now looked a little more humble. Within a matter of minutes, the matter was settled and several traditional favorites had been selected.

''Got it,'' Betty said, slapping a hand on her pleated wool skirt after she'd recorded the decision. ''I'll give this to Emma to type up for the weekly bulletin. Thanks, Ben.''

Ben searched out Sara, who sat rocking Tyler in a oak chair in the corner. She looked as beautiful and maternal as ever. Again he was struck by the perfect picture the woman and child made. And he realized his life wouldn't be complete until they were both in it permanently. On the way home, Ben intended to ask Sara Conroy for a date.

Then, on that date, he intended to ask her to marry him.

Sara checked her makeup one more time, then stood staring off into space, her fingers automatically searching out the cross pendant she wore around her neck. The worry stone centered in the middle of the large wooden cross had sure come in handy lately. Tonight Sara had practically rubbed the polished stone down to a nub.

She didn't know why she was so nervous, but she'd changed clothes at least five times, finally settling on a long, high-necked flared brown wool jersey dress with tight sleeves. The color matched the beaded work in the necklace Ben had given her. And tonight it seemed especially important that she wear the necklace—for hope, for courage, for the strength Ben had assured her the necklace would bring.

She and Ben were going on a date. A real, honest-to-goodness date. Sadie was staying with little Tyler, the weather was brisk and cold, the night clear and bright—no storm predictions, and Ben had had no major crises this week at work. A perfect evening.

Or at least she hoped it would be perfect.

It was two weeks before Christmas. Maybe that was why Sara felt so keyed-up. She'd be leaving Fairweather soon, so she knew this might be the last time she and Ben would have to be alone together. It would be strange, being with him without Tyler. The baby had always served as a gentle buffer against any further intimacy, any further delving into the past or venturing toward an uncertain future.

In all the rest of the times they'd shared, they'd usually been surrounded by co-workers or members of the congregation. No chance to develop a close relationship, other than the mutual friendship they'd both acknowledged. And that had been just fine with Sara, until she'd fallen in love. Ben was right; she'd used everything and everyone as a shield to keep from getting closer to him. She just couldn't bear to fall in love with him and know he'd never be able to return that love.

Now she had to admit she was in love with him. But she still wasn't sure about how he really felt. At times it seemed as if he might feel the same; other times she thought he was just being a good friend, as he'd promised.

Remembering the last time she'd seen Ben, Sara felt the familiar tightness in her heart. She'd only gone to Betty's planning session as a favor to her temporary boss. Betty had insisted they could use Sara's help with the children and that she'd come in handy helping keep things in order as far as food and drink. Sara, not having anything to occupy her once she went home to her own little cottage not too far from Betty's big house, had agreed to help out. Knowing Ben would be there had helped in that decision, she had to admit. She liked being in the same room with him, and she loved taking care of Tyler. Plus she was almost certain Betty knew these things, too, and had wanted to bring them together. Fairweather was full of well-meaning matchmakers.

She could never tell Ben, but she'd become attached to him and Tyler, too—even though she knew Ben's attachment to her was strictly on a friends-only basis—in spite of her imagining otherwise. At Betty and Warren's wedding, she'd hoped things might be changing for Ben and her, but in the weeks since, things had remained the same.

Sara didn't have the nerve to make a move, to tell Ben her true feelings. But now the thought of leaving was tearing through her soul, making her think crazy thoughts. Making her wish she could be all the things Ben needed her to be.

"Just stop," she told herself now as she ran a hand through her upswept riot of unruly curls. "You can be his friend. You can support him in his efforts to adopt Tyler, but that's it. You can't be something you weren't meant to be. No matter how much you want it in your heart."

Sara held her fingers to her cross. She loved her necklace, wore it every day. It was always there, reminding her that she wasn't alone. Reminding her that Ben cared about her…and that God did, too.

She left the bedroom, pacing the small living room until she found herself standing by the windows, looking out toward the frozen lake waters. Over the trees, a million stars twinkled toward her, assuring her that heaven wasn't so far away after all.

Sara stared up into the night sky, then spoke out loud. "Dear God, I know You're up there. You've always been there. And even though I haven't turned to You a lot lately, I'm turning to You now. Ben says You will listen, no matter how long it's been since I prayed. I'm praying now, Lord, for something, something to help me find the strength to go, to leave Fairweather. Help me to make the right choice. Help me to find the strength to walk away from Ben and Tyler. I can't seem to find any other way."

She stopped, her heart racing, her mind whirling.

At least they had tonight. She'd enjoy this quiet time with Ben, cherish it as a sweet memory. She'd appreciate the moment, rejoice in her newfound friend. That would have to be enough.

She didn't deserve to ask for anything more.

An hour later Sara sat with Ben in a secluded restaurant out on the lake. They had a corner table, complete with a spectacular view of the winter wonderland spread out before them. The trees glistened a shimmering gray-blue in the moonlight, while the night sky looked like a dark sheet of navy satin set against the pearly white snow. Out on the wide pier, a brightly lit star shone in white-gold colors, reminding all patrons of the season.

"Ben, this is so nice," she said, gazing across the small round table at him. He looked handsome in his dark wool jacket and white button-down shirt, with the intimate candlelight playing across his face. "And the menu—everything sounds great. I'm hungry."

"They're popular for their steaks and seafood, so order whatever your heart desires. The dessert is good, too." He grinned then waved a hand at the window. "Tonight, the sky's the limit."

"Did you get a bonus?" she teased, her nervousness subsiding just a bit.

"No, but I've got a little tucked back in savings. And since I rarely indulge, I'd say we're entitled."

"It is Christmas."

"Yes, and over the next few weeks I won't have much time to enjoy a quiet dinner such as this one."

"Then I'm all the more pleased you wanted to share it with me."

He grinned again, sapping her calmness in much the same way the winter wind was sapping the stark tree limbs lining the lake. Then he leaned forward, his eyes as velvet-blue as the night. "Did I tell you you look really pretty? I like your hair up like that."

Sara grabbed her cross, rubbing the stone for all it was worth. "It didn't want to cooperate, so I just pulled it up with a clamp."

"I like your uncooperative hair."

"Thank you."

"I see you're wearing the necklace."

Realizing she'd been clinging to it for dear life, Sara dropped her hand in her lap. "Yes. I've had several compliments on it. I tell everyone who asks about it to go to your friend and get one for themselves. Hope he sells lots of these."

Ben shook his head. "I doubt that. It's one of a kind."

"Really?" Shocked and touched, Sara reached for her necklace again. "He only makes originals?"

"He made that one especially for me, or rather

for the special one-of-a-kind person I wanted to give it to."

Sara felt tears pricking at the back of her eyes. "Oh, Ben. That's the sweetest thing anyone's ever done for me. I'll cherish it always."

He took her hand in his. "Just remember what that necklace represents."

"I will, I promise. I'll remember everything you've done for me, too."

"I haven't done anything. I just enjoy being with you, and I want you to understand how much my faith means to me. It's my life."

"I do understand," she told him, her fingers touching on his. "And I appreciate what your faith has taught me about my own. I'm stronger now, from having known you."

"Don't make it seem so final."

"It's not final. We'll stay in touch, I hope."

"I'm planning on that."

She wondered about his smile. It was the same smile he'd given her at Betty and Warren's wedding. She didn't want to misinterpret anything though, so she just accepted it as part of Ben's charm.

The dinner progressed with good food and soft, uninterrupted conversation. The restaurant staff knew exactly when to bring the food and exactly when to leave them alone. When dessert and coffee arrived, Sara felt a sense of regret. This wonderful night would soon be over.

But she soon found out Ben had other thoughts.

He finished the last of his Italian cream cake, then took both of her hands in his. "Sara, there's something I'd like to talk to you about."

The look was back—the expectant, hopeful look. Sara's heart turned to snowflakes inside her chest while her mind battled hope against hope. "Go ahead."

"We're friends, right?"

"Of course."

"And we're compatible."

"I'd say so."

"And you love Tyler as much as I do, right?"

"You know I do."

"And we're both lonely, stuck in limbo, wouldn't you say?"

"I guess so." Wondering where all of this was leading, she laughed shakily. "What are you trying to tell me, Ben?"

Ben lowered his head, closed his eyes, then took a long breath. "I'm making a mess of this, but I've given it a lot of consideration and thought. I think I've found a practical solution that will benefit both of us. We make a good team, we'd make good parents for Tyler, and while we haven't taken things between us beyond friendship, I think we should...I think we should consider getting married."

The silence that followed Ben's proclamation sounded like a snow-covered night—stark, cold and brilliant.

Sara went through an entire gamut of emotions,

starting with surprise, followed by elation, then finally, hurt, indignation and resignation. Ben Hunter had just asked her to marry him.

But he'd never once mentioned that he loved her and wanted her to be his wife.

Chapter Thirteen

Ben waited, his heart skipping a beat as he watched Sara's face. Her first reaction gave him hope, but then her expression changed from open and happy to a pale blank sheet that rivaled the snow lining the window seal.

"Well, what do you think?" he asked, a sinking feeling centering in the middle of his stomach. "It's a practical solution, don't you agree?"

Sara lifted her chin, her eyes misty and wide, a frown creasing her brow. "Practical? Is that your idea of marriage, Reverend?"

Ben knew from the tone in her voice that this wasn't going the way he'd planned. "No. I mean, yes...in this case, yes. We're friends, but a marriage based on friendship can work. At least I think it can."

"You think it can?" She looked away, out over

the snow. Then in a soft voice she said, "I thought all marriages were supposed to be based on love."

Ben didn't speak at first. Should he tell her that he did love her? No, not now. Now she'd just think he wasn't being honest, that he was trying to make up for this big, big mistake. Letting out a breath, he said, "That's true, but a lot of marriages start out with friendship. That's how Betty and Warren started, and now my mother and Reverend Winslow."

"So you decided to throw in with them and take a chance on me?"

"Sara, don't look so sad. Even though you've made it clear that we're just friends, I thought because you care about Tyler and because you're alone, too...I thought you'd at least consider this."

"You don't want to know what I'm considering right now," she told him, her eyes blazing such a deep green, Ben had to blink. "But I'll tell you exactly what I think about your 'practical' solution. I think you only want me as your wife to help you adopt Tyler. I think you only want me as your wife to help your standing within the church. And I think you don't even begin to know the meaning of all those vows you have couples repeat when you perform wedding ceremonies."

Before he could gain the breath to speak, she held up a hand and continued. "Betty and Warren Sinclair are so in love, they light up a room when they enter it. All of our friends are that way, too. In love, Ben. They love each other. They were friends of course, but they were in love before they ever agreed on marriage.''

"Luke and Julianne were friends," he interjected in a rush, "and they agreed to get married just so the twins could have a mother."

Sara scoffed. "Whether either you or Luke realize it, Julianne was half in love with that man when she married him."

"She told you that?"

"She didn't have to tell me. I've heard how they met, what happened to bring them together. What is it with men? Don't you all realize a woman today would never enter into a marriage if she didn't have true feelings for the other person?''

"Well, do you have feelings for me?"

Sara threw her hands up in the air, then sat silent for a long time, as if weighing that particular question. "Right now I don't know how I feel about you. But my answer to your well-thought-out proposal is a big, loud no."

Ben lowered his head. "I'm sorry. I just thought—''

"No, you didn't think," she retorted, anger and hurt bringing out a deep flush against her alabaster skin. "You seem to have forgotten that I was engaged—to a man who couldn't make a firm commitment to me, to a man who wanted everything his way. To a man who left me when the going got tough. Do you honestly think I'd rush into a marriage now...just for convenience?"

Ben didn't know what to say, how to repair the

damage he'd just done. Of course Sara wanted a firm commitment. She wanted more than he had to offer, and she wanted to be able to give her heart completely, which meant she didn't care about him enough to go into a marriage just for the sake of friendship and companionship.

"I guess not," he finally said, his eyes downcast. "Sara, I'm so sorry."

Pushing her chair back, Sara stood. "I'd like to go home now."

Ben reached out a hand to her, gently grabbing her slender arm. "Sara, wait. Let me explain."

"I've heard that line before."

"But…you don't understand."

He'd tell her. Just tell her outright that he loved her. But she didn't love him. She couldn't love him and that was why marriage to him sounded so distasteful. And she'd accused him of some very conniving things. But he had hoped marrying her would help him with the adoption, and having a wife would improve his standing in some people's eyes. While her accusations hurt, they did hit close to home. But he'd never meant it to sound that way.

Telling himself Sara was just upset and that she didn't really believe those things about him, Ben decided he'd done enough damage for one night. Now he'd probably never be able to tell her how he really felt.

Because of her bad experience, she couldn't trust anyone right now. He should have seen that, but he'd been so wrapped up in solving his own dilemma, he'd never stopped to consider how cold and calculating this would seem to Sara.

"I understand more than you'll ever know," Sara said as she swept by him, heading to the front of the restaurant.

Ben hurriedly paid the check to the overly interested hostess who'd been watching the whole scene, then made a mad dash to catch up with Sara.

She was already at the car, waiting, her head down, her arms wrapped against the thick wool of her coat. Ben stopped just before he reached her, wishing he could take back his harebrained plan and just pull her into his arms and tell her what was really on his mind. But it was too late for any declarations of love and truth now.

Silently he opened the car door for her, then drove the short distance around the lake to her cottage. Before he could get out of the car to help her, Sara shot out of her side, then hurried to the front door. "Good night, Ben," she said over her shoulder.

Ben got out and stood there, the slamming of the door echoing through the trees around him with a finality that left him searching for answers and wondering why he'd acted so stupid.

He'd ruined it for both of them. Not only had he managed to mess up the marriage proposal, but he'd probably just lost the best friend a man could ever ask for.

Looking up at the brilliant blanket of stars winking back at him, Ben had never felt so alone in all of his life.

"I hate to leave you like this, Betty," Sara told her supervisor bright and early the next Monday, "but...I have to get back to St. Paul. Right away."

Betty took off her bifocals and leaned back in her desk chair. "Sara, what on earth's happened? You weren't in church yesterday. Is everything okay?"

Seeing the wary concern in Betty's hazel eyes, Sara flinched then looked away. "I—I wasn't feeling very well. And now...well, I'm afraid I can't finish out the next couple of weeks. I won't be able to stay through Christmas. I'm sorry."

Betty made a noise that sounded like a frustrated grunt. "Why don't you tell me what's really going on."

Sara couldn't hide her emotions. She'd tried all weekend. Staying shuttered in her cottage, she'd drank gallons of coffee and stared out at the lake, all the while wondering if she'd been too hasty in turning Ben down.

She'd been so angry, so hurt, that she'd said some things she didn't really mean. She could tell she'd hurt Ben, too, by saying those things. He at least wanted to marry her, even if it was for all the wrong reasons. Or was it for all the right reasons? Little Tyler needed a mother, and Ben needed a helpmate. And she needed both of them in her life because she loved them both so dearly.

Sara just didn't think she had the courage or fortitude to be either a mother or a helpmate right now, though. Because...she couldn't settle for a man who could only offer her friendship, no matter how tempting it would be to fall into Ben's arms. No, if she accepted and married Ben, he'd soon know the truth. She wouldn't be able to hide her feelings and he'd realize she loved him. That could make things awkward, since he obviously couldn't return that love.

"Honey, you look as if you could use a good cry," Betty said now as she came around her desk to place two firm hands on Sara's shoulders. "What happened?"

Sara had fought against the pain, the humiliation, all weekend, but now, with Betty's maternal instincts forcing the issue, she could only slump against the other woman, gulping hard to hold back the inevitable tears.

"Okay, okay." Betty hugged her close, rocking her as if Sarah had just lost a loved one. "Come on over here and sit down on the couch. Then you can explain everything." She pulled Sara along with her, her hand squeezing Sara's in reassurance. "And it won't go any further, I promise."

As if to prove her point, Betty closed the door to the long hallway, effectively shutting away the bright chatter of toddlers and the occasional cry from one of the babies.

Sara sank down on the overstuffed love seat near

the window of Betty's spacious office. "I do need to talk to someone. I guess I need some advice."

"That's part of my job," Betty said, a concerned smile crossing her lips. "But that's also part of being a friend, too. You know, Sara, you've come to mean a lot to all of us around here. Particularly our minister."

Sara gritted her teeth, fighting back the tears. "Are you so sure about that?"

"Ah, Ben." Betty shook her head. "So we get to the gist of the matter. Did you and Ben have a fight?"

Sara shifted, then wiped away an annoying tear. "More like a battle—a strong battle of wills."

"Do you want to talk about it?"

"He asked me to marry him," Sara blurted out, tears rolling down her face.

Betty clapped her hands together. "Well, that's great news. So why are you crying and telling me you have to leave Fairweather?"

Sara shrugged then wiped at her red-rimmed eyes. "Because…because he doesn't love me. He only did it for…for practical purposes. He thinks we're a good team, that we'd be good for Tyler, that it would be a benefit to both of us. A benefit— he makes it sound like an insurance policy!"

"Oh, boy." Betty settled down beside Sara, then took one of her hands in her own, rubbing it as to put the warmth back in it. "Not exactly roses and candlelight, huh?"

Sara shook her head. "He took me to a romantic

dinner out on the lake. We talked, laughed—we had so much fun. Then he asked me to marry him.''

"So far so good. But…something was missing?''

Sara bobbed her head. "Yes, a very big something. Love! I want someone to love, not someone to be my best buddy.''

Betty nodded her understanding. "Well, Ben is an honorable, caring man. I'm sure he thought he was doing the right thing.''

"Right for him, maybe, but not right in my mind. I can't stay here, Betty. I can't face him. I tried so hard to avoid getting too close, getting attached to him and Tyler, and now look at me. I'm a mess.''

"You're in love," Betty stated, slapping a hand on her navy flared skirt. "Happens to the best of us.''

"Well, why did it have to happen to me? I didn't want it to. I wasn't ready for this. It's like being blindsided.''

"Yeah, that's love all right. A glorious thing.''

Sara wiped away her tears, then glared up at Betty. "Not when the man you love can't even bring himself to talk about his past relationship. Betty, Ben's still grieving over Nancy, and he…he hasn't even been able to talk about her with me. He doesn't love me. He can't love anyone else until he comes to terms with her death. I can't imagine being married to someone who pines away for a lost love. It wouldn't be fair to either of us.''

"You have a good point there," Betty agreed,

her tone soothing. "If Ben Hunter has a flaw, it's that he's so busy listening to other people's problems, he's managed to hide his own. He stays busy to block out his grief, and that's caused him to be a little tight-lipped and guarded about his personal life."

Sara felt like one of the toddlers being efficiently placated. "Then you agree he needs to deal with Nancy's death before he can love anyone else?"

"No, I didn't say that. I just said you have a good point. But honey, I think you're missing one really important issue here. Ben Hunter is a man in love."

Sara brought her head up then, her eyes widening as she stared at Betty in disbelief. "Not with me."

"Yes, with you. That poor man's got it so bad, he doesn't know if he's coming or going. He just doesn't know how to convey that to you."

"I don't believe that," Sara said, jumping up to pace the room. "I think Ben cares about me. And he's been a good friend. He's taught me to turn to God in times of need, and to forgive myself for my shortcomings. He's a wonderful person, but until he comes to me himself and tells me that he's over Nancy, until he can bring himself to share that part of his past with me, I won't believe he could ever love me. I have to hear it from him, Betty. I have to know that I'm the one he loves." She stopped ranting, then turned to face the other woman. "Besides, it doesn't really matter anyway. Look at me—do I look like I could possibly be a minister's wife?''

"You look as good as any minister's wife I've ever seen," Betty told her. Getting up, she grabbed Sara by the shoulders again. "That's just downright silly, worrying about that. The good Lord knows you're only human, Sara. None of us is perfect. None of us is above reproach. We just get up each day and do the best we can, with the talents and the guidelines God gave us. And we pray about the rest.''

Sara's sigh shuttered out of her body. "Then pray for me. Pray for Ben. I love him so much, but I can't marry him.''

"I will pray for both of you," Betty told her. "But Sara, think long and hard before you walk away from Ben Hunter. You should tell him how you really feel. You two have a real chance at happiness here, and if you throw that chance away because of pride and misunderstanding, it might be the biggest mistake of your life.''

"It was all a big mistake," Ben told Morgan and Luke as they watched the boys' basketball team running through a practice drill in the church gym. "I messed up, big-time.''

Morgan and Luke exchanged knowing glances as swiftly as they exchanged the basketball back and forth between them.

Morgan caught the ball, then held it near his stomach with one arm. "Well, my friend, I have to admit your intentions were honorable, but it sounds like you went about it all wrong."

Ben nodded, then turned to Luke. "But you didn't love Julianne when you two got married. You wanted a mother for your children."

Luke shrugged, then sighed. "Well, I told myself that at the time, but let's face it—Julianne and I were attracted to each other from the first, just like you and Sara. And I think she was more receptive to the idea because I had children and she didn't think she'd ever be able to have any of her own."

"That's changed now," Morgan said, grinning as he tapped his friend on the shoulder. "We're both in the family way, in a big way."

Ben felt that familiar tug of envy, coupled with joy for both of his friends. They'd announced earlier that they were going to have new babies in their households in a few months. "I'm happy for both of you, by the way, even if I've managed to ruin my own chances at being a husband and father."

Luke grinned right back. "A lot of things have changed now. But Julianne and I soon realized we loved each other. Maybe from the beginning."

Morgan glanced over at Ben, then tossed him the ball. "Which is the case with you and Sara, I believe."

Ben shuffled, dribbled the ball, then tossed it back to Morgan. "I know how *I* feel, but Sara doesn't love me. She's made that clear. And she also made it very clear that she won't marry a man she doesn't love. She has always stressed that we can only be friends, and now I guess I won't even have her friendship to count on.''

"Do you love this woman?" Luke asked in a mock-stern voice, his eyes twinkling in spite of the serious question.

Before answering, Ben blew the whistle, then called to the boys. "That's enough for today. Go shower and get home. Be on time for warm-up before Friday's game."

"He's stalling," Morgan said as he watched the stomping feet of sweaty adolescents roar by like a herd of gazelles.

Ben waited until the locker room door banged shut, then turned back to his friends. "I didn't want the kids to overhear. Everyone around here's already involved enough in my personal life as it is."

"Which is why we're waiting for an answer," Luke told him, tapping a sneakered foot in impatience. "But I think we all already know the answer."

Ben hung his head, then lifted his gaze to his friends. "Yes, I love her. But I didn't have the nerve to tell her that."

Morgan poked Ben in the stomach. "Well, tell her now. I mean, what can be worse at this point? Letting her leave thinking you only wanted to marry her for—what did you call it?—'practical purposes,' or asking her to stay because you really love her and want to make a life with her and Tyler?"

"I vote for the second choice," Luke said, adding his own encouraging poke to Morgan's. "If you don't tell Sara the truth, she might leave for good and you'll never know what might have been."

Ben looked up then, a shining light of realization clicking on in his head, in his heart. "What might have been? Ever since Nancy died, I've asked myself that question at least ten times a day. I think I've been so worried with *what might have been,* that I've failed to see the possibilities of what *could be.*"

Morgan and Luke glanced at each other again.

"I think he's catching on," Luke stated, nodding his approval. "You know, Reverend, you preach a mean sermon, but you don't follow your own advice."

Ben lifted the basketball toward the nearby net, making a perfect free throw shot. "Well, I intend to do just that from now on."

"Two points." Morgan hooted, then slapped Ben on the back. "Go for it."

"I am," Ben told them. "I'm going to tell Sara the truth, and place the rest of it in God's hands."

"Now you're talking," Luke replied, his grin back.

Ben looked up at his buddies. "Thanks. I really appreciate both of you listening to my sob story."

"Don't make a habit of it," Luke told him, grinning. Then with his expression changing, he added, "You've helped both of us through some tough times, Ben. It's only fair that we do the same for you—when you'll let us."

Ben laughed then. "I'll have to remember that sometimes the preacher himself needs to hear a good lesson on life."

"That's what we're here for," Morgan said as they headed toward the locker rooms.

Just then they heard the door opening on the other side of the gym. All three men turned to find Emma rushing toward them, her heels clicking on the polished wood, a look of concern on her face.

"Reverend, come quick," she called, her voice breathless and shrill. "It's Tyler. Something's wrong—he's sick. Sara says we need to rush him to the hospital right away."

Chapter Fourteen

"Morgan, you have to tell me what's going on in there."

Ben paced the small area just outside the emergency room, still in his sweats and sneakers. Sara sat in a chair beside the room where they'd taken Tyler earlier, and all around, anxious church members stood in clusters, supporting Ben in his time of need.

Morgan, who'd driven Ben and the baby to the emergency room and asked his fellow pediatricians if he could help with the examination, had now come out of the examining room, his expression grim.

Morgan placed a gentle hand of restraint on Ben's arm. "They're doing everything they can to bring the fever down, but Ben, I have to be honest with you. They think it might be meningitis."

Sara jumped up, a hand going to her heart. "I was afraid of that. I've seen it too many times. The rash, the high fever." Her voice became shaky. "And when I couldn't get him to respond, when he wouldn't wake up, I just knew."

"You did the right thing, alerting us," Morgan told her. "We got him here quickly for treatment and that could very well make all the difference."

Ben grabbed his friend's arm. "You mean, that could save his life? Is Tyler going to die, Morgan?"

Morgan glanced from one anxious face to the other. "I don't want to mislead you. It's serious. But Ben, we have advanced treatment and medication now that we didn't have years ago, and as soon as we can determine whether it's bacterial or viral, we'll be able to help him more."

"How will you do that? How soon will we know?" Ben ran a nervous hand through his hair. "What are they doing in there?"

"They're going to do a spinal tap," Morgan explained.

Ben didn't miss the look Morgan gave Sara. "Is that painful? Will it hurt him?"

Sara spoke at last. "He has to lie completely still, Ben. It's just a prick, but it looks much worse to those watching than it feels for the baby."

"I want to go in there," Ben said, heading for the room.

Morgan pulled him back. "I don't think that's a very good idea. We don't know how contagious this is yet. The doctors know what they're doing, Ben. He'll be just fine.''

Ben turned to Sara. ''Then you go. You're a nurse. You're trained for this. Sara, please, go in and hold him while they do the test.''

Sara shot Morgan a misty-eyed look. ''Will it be okay?''

''Sure.'' Morgan nodded, then indicated his head toward the room. ''I'll go back in, too. Together we'll make sure Tyler doesn't have to suffer any undue pain.''

Ben felt Sara's hand on his arm. ''Ben, is that all right with you?''

Seeing the doubt and concern in her eyes, Ben regained some of his composure. As scared as he was, he didn't want to worry Sara. She loved Tyler, too. ''Of course. Thank you.''

''We'll take good care of him,'' Morgan told him as he guided Sara into the room.

Ben stood watching her walk away, thinking how happy he'd been just over an hour ago. His decision to tell Sara the truth had been liberating, setting him free from three long years of guilt and isolation. He'd realized so much, standing in that chilly gym with his friends, the sound of kids playing basketball all around.

He now knew that as much as he loved Sara, he'd been holding part of himself away from that love—out of respect for Nancy's memory. He'd believed that it would be dishonorable to love someone else, when he'd never quite gotten over losing her. But Ben knew Nancy would be upset if he didn't find someone to share his life with. She'd been that kind of woman—giving, nurturing, putting others above herself, so much like Sara, yet so different, too.

Ben had attempted to keep that part of Nancy alive, by trying to be all the things she'd expected him to be, all the things that had made her proud of him. But all of his efforts had been a sham, really, because he'd guarded his heart to the point of becoming a kind of detached observer. Until Tyler. Until Sara.

He didn't want to be an observer anymore. He wanted to participate in life—good or bad.

No, to turn away from a chance at happiness wouldn't help to honor Nancy's memory, it would just make him even more bitter and lonely, and that would be a disgrace to her spirit, her love, everything they'd shared together.

After talking to his friends, and now with Tyler so ill, all of Ben's worries, his fears about loving too much had been washed away. He did love too much, so much that it hurt to think of life without Tyler and Sara. If only he'd had the courage to tell Sara the truth the other night, things might be so different right now.

Now, though, he wouldn't be able to tell Sara about his revelation, about how much he wanted to make her his wife. Now he had to put Tyler first.

"Dear God, he has to be all right."

Ben didn't even realize he'd said the prayer out loud until he turned to find Betty's hand on his arm.

"Here, Ben, take some coffee. You look drained. Want me to send Warren to the cafeteria for some supper?"

"I can't eat," he told her, accepting the coffee if only to warm his cold hands. "He has to be okay, Betty. That little baby's been through so much, and…"

"Don't think about it," Betty told him. "God will see us through this, Ben."

"But what if he dies?"

Betty patted him on the back, her touch gentle and motherly. "If Tyler dies, we'll just have to accept that God needed him in Heaven more than we needed him here on earth."

Shocking himself and Betty, Ben said, "I don't know if I can accept that. I don't know anymore, Betty. Maybe this is my lesson, for being so callous, for being so smug in my advice, when I didn't really even begin to know what I was talking about. Why would God send that little boy to me, then turn around and take him away?"

Ben saw the anxiety in Betty's hazel eyes, saw the uncertainty in her expression. "I don't have an answer for that," she told him, her voice soft but firm. "But we're going to think positive, and hope we don't have to wonder why."

Ben slumped into a nearby chair, his every prayer centered on Tyler. He was so grateful for Sara being here. Just knowing she was in there with

Tyler, soothing him, talking to him, made Ben feel better.

He glanced around, amazed at the support Tyler was receiving from the church. Betty and Warren, Luke, Sadie, Emma, Maggie and Frank, and several other church members had all poured in, and now were keeping a constant vigil. Julianne and Rachel had stayed at home with the twins, Rachel's daughter, Lindsay, and Maggie's little Elizabeth Anne. Since they didn't know what Tyler had yet, Julianne and Rachel couldn't expose their unborn babies to a risk. Luckily none of the children in Julianne's class had been exposed.

Ben closed his eyes, sending up a prayer of thanks. This community always pulled together, helping each other when times were tough. He'd seen that all this year, from last Christmas, to Lent, then the beautiful Easter service last spring, to the tornadoes of this summer, and in the many festivals and celebrations, to the times they'd all gathered right here in this hospital to celebrate births and mourn deaths.

But Ben couldn't—wouldn't—mourn the death of one so young, so innocent, so treasured.

He prayed silently now, his eyes shut to the pain. When he felt a warm hand in his, Ben opened his eyes to find Sadie kneeling beside his chair, her thick sable-colored curls framing her ageless face.

"Keep praying, Reverend Ben," she said, her dark eyes bright with assurance, her grip on his hand tightening. "We're all here."

Ben glanced around to see his friends and fellow church members joining hands to form a circle. He felt both humbled and blessed to know that these people cared about Tyler and him so much. So he stood, holding on to Sadie's sturdy, steady hand on one side, and Betty's firm grip on the other. Then he opened his heart and prayed out loud.

"Dear Lord, please help us to understand. Help us to bear the burden. Help little Tyler, God. He's an innocent, brought to us through Your grace and assurance. And he's taught all of us so much—how to love unconditionally, how to overcome our own burdens and troubles and put others' needs before our own. This baby has brought our church together and brought this ministry the support and love that You've taught us to give. Lord, I ask in Your Name, please protect, watch over, heal…my son. Amen."

Ben smelled the fragrance that always brought him joy, then opened his eyes to find Sara standing there in front of him in hospital scrubs, her hand reaching for his, her eyes bright with glistening tears.

"They just finished the spinal tap, Ben," she said, her voice so soft, so gentle, he thought maybe he was dreaming. "We should know something soon."

While they waited for the results of the test, the doctors went ahead and put Tyler on antibiotics. Almost certain it was meningitis, they didn't want to take any chances. The night dragged on and soon the group of watchers dwindled, but Ben and Sara stayed near Tyler's bedside.

Although they didn't talk much, the silence was not entirely uncomfortable to Sara. She didn't press Ben for conversation. He seemed centered on watching over Tyler, centered in prayer and meditation. Out of respect, she allowed him his silence. Out of pain and fear, she refrained from voicing her own thoughts.

But Sara refused to leave. She wanted so much to take Ben in her arms and tell him how much she truly loved him, but now was not the time. Now they could only wait and hope. And if the worst happened, she'd be right here. Ben needed to know that she wouldn't desert him even during the darkest of times, even if he couldn't share his worst fears with her. After all, wasn't that the truest measure of unconditional love?

The dawn came. Tyler had survived the night. And Sara had learned the greatest lesson of all.

"He had a cold and then he had a couple of ear infections," Sara told Maggie early the next morning. "That's why he was fussy all those times. I knew that, but I never thought about the possibility of meningitis. I should have monitored him better."

"You had no way of knowing it could turn into this," Maggie said. "Morgan told us last night that meningitis develops within twenty-four hours. So, none of us could have predicted this."

Sara took the bag of cinnamon rolls Maggie had picked up at Swenson's Bakery, laying them on a nearby table. "But yesterday, I was so…distracted. He was fussy again, and I tried to comfort him, but then—" She closed her eyes, remembering how still Tyler had been when she'd gone to get him ready to go home with Ben. So quiet, so still, so burning hot with fever. "I've never been so scared in all of my life. He could have died."

Maggie took Sara's hand in her own. "Well, he didn't. And Morgan said the fever seems to be slowly going down. The first night is always the most critical, and he made it through."

"The longest night of my life," Sara told her, glancing up to where Ben sat sleeping in a nearby armchair. Motioning toward him, she whispered, "He's exhausted, but he won't leave. He's paced the floor most of the night—that is, when he wasn't in there, watching over Tyler. He loves that little boy."

"And you love both of them," Maggie stated, a compassionate expression crossing her face. "Why don't you tell him? He could use some good news right now."

"I can't," Sara whispered, afraid Ben would wake. "Not now. Maybe not ever. We had a terrible fight the other night and I've made such a mess of things. I've hurt him with my angry words and awful accusations."

Thankfully Maggie didn't push her for details.

"I'm sure Ben knows you didn't really mean anything bad you might have said."

"No, I didn't mean any of it. It's just so hard. I need to talk to him, but he's got enough to deal with without me handing over all my baggage, too."

Maggie wrapped a comforting arm around Sara's shoulder. "Well, at least you're still here. That shows him you care."

"I couldn't desert him and Tyler, not when I was the one responsible for Tyler's well-being. If I hadn't been so upset and miserable yesterday, I might have seen this sooner. But I was too busy wallowing in self-pity."

"Stop blaming yourself," Maggie admonished. "Stay here as long as you need to. I can pinch-hit for you back at the nursery. And Sadie's offered her help, too. She's there right now, taking in the early arrivals. Morgan's going to stop by there, to check out the babies who were exposed to whatever Tyler might have."

"I didn't even consider that," Sara said, a long sigh moving through her body. "I'm sure Betty has that well in hand, though."

"She's like a drill sergeant—and I'm sure all the other babies are just fine. Betty has always abided by the strictest of sanitary rules, anyway. And Morgan will spot anything unusual in the other children." She sighed, then patted Sara's hand. "Betty will mainly want to keep the other parents from going into a panic."

"And you'll be there to help, too."

"Yes." Maggie gave her a reassuring nod. "I kinda miss the old place, anyway."

"Are you sure you don't mind?"

"Very. Especially since Betty told me you might have to leave town earlier than expected. This will give me a chance to polish up my rusty skills."

Worried that Betty had broken her pledge to keep Sara's explanation confidential, Sara gave Maggie a worried look. "I hope you understand."

"Not really, and no, Betty didn't bother explaining the details, but since you just told me Ben and you had a disagreement, I get the distinct impression it has to do with the adorable man sleeping in that chair over there."

"It's all so complicated," Sara admitted. "But I can't leave Ben now. And I certainly won't leave until I know Tyler is going to be all right."

"We're all praying for that," Maggie said, raising up out of her chair. "Now, I'm going to work and you try to get some rest. And call us as soon as you hear anything different, good or bad."

"I will."

After Maggie left, Sara sat there in the silence of early morning, watching Ben as he dozed. She loved him so very much, and this latest crisis had only reinforced that love. Sitting here now, she made a silent pledge to God.

Let me have one more chance, Lord. Let Ben ask me again—to marry him. This time I'll say yes, because I can't live without him in my life. That's all

I ask—one more chance. This time I won't be too harsh or hasty in giving my answer. This time I'll say yes. Please, Lord.

Silently she prayed for Tyler and Ben, asking God to help them both. And if God saw fit to take Tyler home, she would be here to help Ben through the pain of losing the child they'd both come to love so much.

After all, she thought, tears of happiness and despair streaming down her face, God had found her again and brought her here. She couldn't leave. She didn't want to leave. She felt that now with such assurance, that it made all of her doubts and fears seem small and insignificant.

Touching on the cross necklace Ben had given her, Sara once again found comfort in the polished stone of her worry rock. The Lord was right there with her; He'd been there all along, in her heart. All she had to do was reach out. She was willing to do that now. Willing to take a risk on being a minister's wife, no matter how hard that task might be, willing to take a risk on helping Ben adopt Tyler, no matter the outcome.

And somehow she had to make Ben see that she loved him, that she could help him get over Nancy, that she would try her best to be a proper wife to him. In time, maybe he would come to love her just as much. They could have a good life together, if only God would give her another chance to make it so.

"When Tyler is better," she said to herself as

she dried her tears. "When Tyler is better, I'll tell Ben the truth."

With that thought in mind, she sat there, clutching her hand to her necklace, her eyes never leaving the man across the room.

Ben woke with a start, his head and heart pounding protest throughout a body that hadn't enjoyed sleeping in a cramped chair all night. Sitting straight up, he remembered why he was here.

Tyler.

Tyler was very sick.

And where were all the doctors?

Glancing around, he saw Sara curled up in a chair across the room, her hand wrapped around her cross necklace, her eyes closed in either sleep or silent prayer. The early-morning sunshine streaming in through the wide glass doors highlighted her like a spotlight.

And that glowing light shone bright and clear to Ben.

She was beautiful. Her dark red hair, tousled by a night spent in such a state, shimmered down her neck and around her shoulders like burnished copper. Her skin, so pale, so dotted with cute freckles, looked alabaster and fragile, like fine porcelain. Her hands, so dainty, so strong, held tight to the thread of her faith.

She'd stayed.

She hadn't abandoned him.

For the first time in many hours, Ben felt a new

hope. Everything would be all right. Tyler would be fine. And then Ben would go to Sara and ask her to marry him again.

Only, this time, he'd make her see that he really meant it. He'd ask her because he loved her with all his heart and he wanted her in his life forever. He'd ask her because she would make a wonderful mother for Tyler, because she loved the baby as much as Ben did. He'd ask her because he no longer had a choice in the matter. Because he was in love. And he now had the courage to tell Sara that.

Lifting his sore, twisted body away from the chair, Ben swept a hand through his hair, determined to find Tyler's doctor to see how the baby was doing.

He didn't have to search long. One of the pediatricians came toward him, a tight-lipped smile plastered on his face. "Ben, we got the results back. It's viral meningitis, which, while it is serious, isn't nearly as serious as bacterial meningitis."

Ben let out a quick breath of thankfulness. "So that means he's going to be all right?"

"I think so, but we're going to have to wait and see. The antibiotics are just a precaution, but they really can't help viral meningitis. It has to run its course. And his fever is down this morning, so we expect a complete recovery. He'll just need a few days of quiet and rest."

"Thank you, Doctor," Ben told the other man, shaking his hand. "Can I see him now?"

"Sure. In fact, he'll need loved ones around to comfort him. He's going to feel pretty uncomfortable over the next few days. Which is why we'll want to keep him here for a while longer."

"I understand," Ben told him. "I won't be far away."

"Neither will I," Sara said, coming up behind Ben. "We can take turns. Want me to take the first shift?"

Ben thanked the departing doctor again, then turned to Sara. "Thank you, I'd appreciate that. But you've already been here all night. You look tired. Are you sure?"

Sara touched his arm. "I'm very sure. I can get some rest sitting by his bed, while you go home and get a shower and check in at the church. I'll be fine. Maggie brought me some breakfast earlier, and Betty called to say she'll bring us some more provisions at lunch."

Ben took her hand, holding it between them. "Sara, I really appreciate this—I mean, after the other night—"

Sara put a finger to his lips. "We're not going to talk about the other night. Right now, Tyler is our main concern, okay?"

He looked down at their joined hands. "You're right. I hope the worst of it is over."

"Now that the doctors know what it is, they can treat it accordingly," she told him. Then, "Ben, I'm so sorry—I should have been more aware. I should have done more for him."

"Hush," he said, unable to resist taking her in his arms. Hugging her close, he whispered, "You have given Tyler the best, the very best care, in the world. If anyone's to blame here, it's me. I was responsible for his well-being, but I passed him around like he was a toy, letting others take care of him when I should have been there."

"You've been a good foster father," Sara said, lifting away from him to gaze up at him. "Don't ever doubt that. These things just happen sometimes. We have to hope that it's a mild case and that he'll pull through with flying colors."

Ben nodded, then touched a hand to her cheek. "When this is all over, we need to get a few things straight, all right?"

"All right."

She smiled up at him, giving him renewed hope. Her eyes were a bright, shining green, expectant and sure.

Ben's heart soared. Maybe, just maybe, Sara would reconsider and marry him in spite of his shortcomings. Maybe everything would turn out all right for them after all.

Emma came bustling through the doors then, her gaze searching out Ben. "Oh, there you are. Thank goodness I found you. How's Tyler?"

Ben told her what they'd just heard.

"Thank the Lord." Then she touched a hand to her upswept hair. "Ben, I forgot to tell you in all the excitement. Last night Jason Erickson called right before closing time, looking for you."

Ben lifted his head, then gave Emma an encouraging nod. Hoping she had her information right, he asked, "What did he say?"

Emma looked a bit confused, then replied, "He said he needed to talk with you, and I told him you were here—that you'd had to rush little Tyler to the hospital." Shrugging, she added, "It was the weirdest thing. He kept asking me what was wrong with the baby. He seemed really upset, maybe because he couldn't talk to you."

"Probably," Ben agreed, wishing he hadn't missed Jason's call. "Thanks, Emma. Did he give any indication as to where he might be?"

She shook her head. "No. He just sounded so...agitated, and then before I could talk to him any further, he hung up on me. My heart goes out to that boy."

"Mine, too," Ben replied, a new source of worrying clouding his earlier hopes. "Maybe he'll call back. I sure hope so. If he's in trouble, he'll need us more than ever."

A couple of hours later, Ben found out just how much Jason needed help. Ben had just returned to Tyler's room, after spending a couple of hours at the church, fielding concerned phone calls and checking in with Emma to make sure she had his pager number, so if Jason did call again, he could reach Ben at the hospital.

He and Sara were standing on either side of Tyler's crib, talking quietly while Tyler slept. The fever had gone down, but Tyler was still fussy and listless, so the doctors were being cautious and watchful.

Ben was trying to convince Sara to go home and get some real sleep, when the door burst open.

Ben and Sara both looked up in surprise to find Jason Erickson and his parents standing there. The look on Jason's face shocked Ben into action.

"Jason?" Ben crossed the space between them to embrace the teen. Although skinnier and haggard-looking, Jason was as handsome as ever, his light brown hair clipped and jutting around his frowning face, his blue eyes bright with a frantic, worried light. "Thank goodness you're home."

But Jason didn't seem to even hear Ben. His eyes were centered on little Tyler. Pushing past Ben, the young man reached the small bed, then glanced across at Sara with a wild gaze. "Is he all right? Is Tyler going to be all right?"

"We think so," Sara told him, wondering why the baby's situation had affected the teenager so much.

"You have to be sure," Jason said, turning to Ben as tears streamed down his face. "Reverend Ben, you have to make sure he's going to be all right."

Clearly confused and concerned, Ben glanced at Richard and Mary Erickson. They looked drained and pale, but as stern and unyielding as ever.

"He insisted we bring him here," Richard tried to explain with a shrug and a sigh.

"What's going on?" Ben asked, his gaze moving from them back to Jason. "Jason?"

Jason whirled away from the bed, his contorted expression showing all the misery in his soul. "Please, don't let him die." Then he fell against Ben, grabbing Ben's shirt with clenched, white-knuckled fists. "Tyler belongs to Patty and me. He's my son, Reverend Ben. Tyler is my son."

Chapter Fifteen

Ben felt as if he'd been physically hit by a fist right in his midsection. Standing back, he held his hands up to Jason, taking the boy by the arms to stare down into his face. "What did you say?"

Jason sniffed back a sob, then gave Ben a wide-eyed look. "Tyler is my son. That's...that's why I had to run away. I had to take care of Patty. She was pregnant."

Richard Erickson huffed a long breath, then slowly shook his head, his expression filled with shock. "I can't believe this is happening—not to my son. Jason, did you forget everything your mother and I taught you?"

Jason whirled to glare at his father then. "No, Father, I didn't forget, and I knew you wouldn't, either. I was afraid, so I ran. I tried to do the right thing, only everything got so mixed up."

Ben looked at Sara. The same despair he felt centered like a heavy stone in his own heart, was reflected in her eyes. All of his earlier hopes now seemed as remote as what Jason had just told him.

Needing to hear the whole story, Ben motioned to the Ericksons. "Let's find somewhere to talk, somewhere private."

"We don't have anything to discuss," Richard told him, his tone stilted, his eyes blazing. "Come on, Jason. We're taking you back home to explain this."

"No, Father," Jason said, a fresh batch of tears cresting in his eyes. "I need to tell Reverend Ben everything, why I couldn't tell him before. I—I had to come home to see if Tyler was going to live. I was so afraid God was punishing him, because of my actions."

Mary rushed to her son, taking the boy in her arms. "Oh, no, no, baby. God wouldn't do that. You can't believe that. Tyler is an innocent child."

"Your son needs help," Ben told Richard Erickson, his own heart filling with such a deep pain, it hurt to take a breath. "Can't you see what he's been through?"

Erickson nodded slowly, then turned toward the door like a sleepwalker.

Ben lifted his head toward Sara.

"I'll stay with him," she said, her expression worried. "Ben?"

He pivoted at the door, one hand on Jason's arm.

"I'm so sorry. I'll pray that everything turns out all right."

"Thank you."

Ben knew what she was trying to convey. If Tyler was an Erickson, what chance would Ben have of adopting him now?

After one of the nurses had escorted them into a private conference room down the hall from the hospital nursery, Ben shut the door and turned to the three people clustered around the small table. "Let's sit down."

Mary slumped into a chair, with Jason soon following. Ben watched as she grasped her son's hand, her misty gaze reassuring Jason, even while her lips quivered.

Richard Erickson let out another sigh, his features as gray and as pale as stone. Finally he threw his expensive overcoat on a nearby chair and sat down.

Ben found a chair and settled wearily into it, his gaze fixed on Jason. "Jason, why don't you start at the beginning. Tell us everything and don't be afraid. We're not here to judge you."

Jason shot his father a look that said he wasn't so sure about that, but he swallowed back his obvious fear and started talking, his voice shaky, his movements nervous.

"Patty and I met back last year when we all went on that youth trip—remember?"

Ben nodded. So far, Emma's story had been accurate. "Why didn't you ever tell me about her?"

Ben again glanced at his father. Shrugging, he said, "At first, we were just friends. But then, the more we talked...well, Patty seemed so interested in me, and she was so sweet, so alone. We really liked each other." Gaining strength, he said, "I didn't want anyone to know about us though, especially my parents."

Richard started to speak, but Ben held up a hand. "Let him explain, Mr. Erickson."

Jason lowered his head, then placed his hands together on the table. "Patty was from another town, so we couldn't really see much of each other at first. I e-mailed her a lot. One of her friends had a computer, so she'd send me messages that way. Then I called her some, too. We started getting together—she had to sneak out and...so did I."

Richard pounded the table with a curled fist, but he kept quiet, his glaring eyes never leaving his son's face.

"I knew you wouldn't approve," Jason finally said, staring across at his father. "That's why I didn't tell anybody, not even Reverend Ben. She wasn't the kind of girl you wanted me to date."

Mary held Jason's hand again. "What kind of girl is Patty?" she asked, her words hesitant and whisper soft.

"She's poor," Jason explained. "Her mother's had a hard time, and her father beats both of them."

Mary gasped, while Richard pursed his lips and

looked down at his shoes. "Well, you're right about that. While I feel for the girl's plight, we'd never allow you to become involved with someone such as this. There are much more suitable girls for you, when the time comes for that sort of thing."

His every word indicated that he didn't think this was the time. On a softer note, he added, "You're still so young, Jason. How could you let something like this happen?"

Jason appealed to his mother then. "I know what we did was wrong, but I loved her, Mother. I mean, *I* thought we were in love. But things got so complicated. I didn't know what to do."

"You slept with her!" Richard got up to stomp around the room. "Son, you know we taught you better!"

Jason jumped up, too. "Yes, Father. You taught me right from wrong, but I was confused and lonely and Patty seemed to really care about me. She listened to my dreams. She understood how lonely I was. I thought she really cared about me. I can see it was wrong, so wrong, but it was too late. She got pregnant."

"So you decided to run away together?" Ben urged Jason back down. "Why didn't you come to me?"

"I wanted to," Jason told him. "But I knew what would happen. I knew you'd want me to tell them." He pointed toward his father. "I didn't want to disappoint *him*."

Mary put a hand to her mouth. "Oh, Jason. Don't you know we would have helped you?"

Jason lifted his chin, his eyes on his father. "No, I didn't know that. I was so scared, so ashamed, I figured you'd be so disappointed in me, you'd probably turn me out anyway."

"*I* wouldn't have done that," Mary told him, her look defiant and tragic.

"I was ashamed and confused, Mother. So I decided to take Patty away, so we could have our baby together. I had some money from my savings account and my allowance money. I thought that would get us started. But Patty had other ideas."

"What kind of ideas?" Richard asked, whirling around to grip the back of his chair.

"She knew my family had money, so she kept insisting that I bring her back to Fairweather. But I told her we couldn't come back here. So we decided to run. She knew a few people in the city, so we headed there first. We stayed in shelters here and there, under different names, and we got help from a few homeless people. I even found some work, just to get money for food and hotel rooms, but it was hard, living that way."

Mary started sobbing, but Richard just stared down at his son, his obvious disappointment throbbing right along with the pulse in his jaw. "I can't believe—"

"I couldn't believe it, either, Father. But I tried to take care of Patty. But it just got worse. We fought constantly, and I soon realized that she didn't feel the same way about me. She didn't have any money, and she didn't have a good family life. She thought because I was rich, I could change all of that. She thought my life was perfect, compared to hers."

"A gold digger," Richard shouted, his face turning beet-red. "You let a little gold digger entice you, and now look where it's brought you."

Jason ran a hand through his hair, then shouted back at his father. "Patty wasn't like that, at least not at first. It's just that she's never had all the luxuries I've had, and she couldn't understand why we couldn't come back here and eventually get married—raise the baby here."

He raised his face toward his father again. "I couldn't make her see that I had disgraced the Erickson name, that I'd never be welcome in my own home again. So we fought all the time before the baby was born. Then after Tyler came along, it got even worse. We had to have formula for the baby, we had to keep him warm and dry. We were running out of options."

He let out a long sigh, then sniffed again. "But in the end, Patty gave up the idea of having a better life with me and she did the only thing she could do. She brought Tyler here to Reverend Ben."

Ben looked up in shock. "You mean, *you* didn't bring Tyler to us?"

"No." Jason shook his head, then looked back down at the table. "We were staying in this shelter near St. Paul. Patty had Tyler in a free clinic, but we left before they could find out our real names and track down our relatives." He slumped over the table, his head in his hands. "It was hard on the baby. Hard on all of us. I wanted to come home, to bring Tyler home, but I was so afraid and mixed-up. We found a temporary shelter and decided we'd try to find work—enough to earn the money to maybe come home.

"For a while, things were okay. We saved up some money, but one day I woke up and Patty and Tyler were gone. The shelter supervisor gave me a note from Patty that said she'd taken Tyler to a safe place and that she was going to Wisconsin to live with her sister. She'd used all of the money to get away." He turned to Ben then. "I called you a few days later, and that's when I found out you had Tyler. I can't tell you how thankful I was for that."

"I remember the call," Ben said on a quiet note. "I just wished you'd told me that Tyler was your son. I would have come and brought you home." Reaching out a hand, he touched Jason's arm. "Jason, I'm proud of you for trying to do what you thought was right, but I'm sure glad you're home and safe."

Richard sent his chair crashing against the table. "You're proud! That's typical of what I'd expect from you, Reverend Hunter. Condoning the boy for his sinning ways. Well, I'm not so proud. I'm not so proud at all."

Jason stood up then, his own rage spilling forth. "No, Father, you were never proud of anything I tried to do. That's why I knew I had to get away. And all this time you've blamed everyone else for this.'' He held up a hand, tears brimming in his eyes again. ''Will you please listen to *me?*''

Richard could only nod his head, his hands still gripping his chair, his eyes blazing his indignation.

''After I found out Tyler was safe with Reverend Ben, I made a promise to God. I promised to work hard to get enough money to come home and face the consequences of my actions, just the way you and Reverend Ben have always taught me to do. I called Reverend Ben and I wanted to tell him everything, but I knew Tyler was better off with him. I also got in touch with Patty at her sister's house, and she told me she didn't want to raise Tyler, that she wasn't ready to be a mother yet. She said that she remembered me talking about Reverend Ben and how he'd forgive anybody and give them a second chance, just like Jesus did. So that's why she brought Tyler to him.''

He stared up at his father again. ''Patty did the best thing. I mean, she could have dumped Tyler on *your* doorstep, or she could have demanded money from you, but she didn't. In spite of everything, she loves Tyler, too, and she knew he'd be safe with Reverend Ben. She's agreed to sign away her rights, and her sister is backing her on that.''

Richard threw up his hands. ''So we're forced to deal with this scandal on our own.''

Mary stood up then, her slight frame shaking. ''*This* scandal happens to involve your son and your grandson, Richard. Or have you even stopped to think about that? Tyler is an Erickson. And he is our grandchild.'' Gaining stamina, she glared at her husband. "Can't you be thankful that Jason is home again? Can't you see past your reputation and what others might judge, to realize that God had brought our child back to us? Or do you want Jason back out there, alone and afraid, simply because *you* can't deal with the scandal?''

Shocked at his diminutive wife's outburst, Richard sank down in his chair again. "Mary, please don't cry. What am I supposed to do about this? Would somebody please tell me?''

Jason sat back down, too. "I'll tell you what I want, Father. I want Tyler to stay with Reverend Ben. I already know Reverend Ben wants to adopt him, and I'm willing to let him.''

Richard Erickson looked at his son, disbelief evident on his face. "You can't be serious. Let *him* adopt *my* grandson? That's ludicrous and completely out of the question.''

Ben spoke then. "It wasn't so ludicrous a minute ago, when you were worried about the scandal. Would you really rather put Jason and Tyler through this, than see me raising that little boy? Do you dislike me so much?''

"He doesn't care about me or Tyler,'' Jason interjected, pointing a finger at his father. "He just wants to control things, like he's always done.''

"That will be enough!'' Richard shouted, banging the table again.

"No, Father," Jason said, his voice calm now. "I don't mean to disrespect you, but it's not enough. It's never been enough. Do you know how many times I longed to play catch with you in the backyard? Do you? But Ericksons don't play catch—not dignified enough. Do you know how many times I wished you'd let me call you Dad instead of Father? But we have to be formal about everything, including our titles for each other. And you never once came to watch me play basketball, did you? No, you always had a meeting or a dinner engagement. You didn't have time to see me wasting my time, as you used to tell me. Can't you see, Father? I don't want Tyler to grow up that way, I want him to be able to play baseball or basketball, and go on field trips and…I want him to be able to call someone Dad."

He stopped, caught his breath, then shook his head. "I am responsible for my actions. I chose to be with Patty. But now I see that I made a big mistake. But Tyler shouldn't have to suffer because of that mistake. I'm not ready to accept the responsibility of being a father, but I can accept the responsibility of making sure Tyler is safe and loved. I want Reverend Ben to go ahead and adopt him."

Lowering his head again, he said on a soft voice, "And maybe someday, I can explain to Tyler why I had to let him go—that is, if God sees fit to let him live. That's why I had to come back. I just felt so responsible, like God was teaching me a lesson."

Ben grabbed Jason then, pulling the boy into his arms, his own eyes burning with unshed tears. "No, Jason. Don't think that. God isn't trying to get even with you. You made a mistake, but you've more than owned up to that mistake. Tyler won't suffer—we have to believe that. He's already better. The doctors told me that earlier this morning. We have to pray that he'll pull through and be on the mend soon."

Jason clung to Ben's sweater. "Are you sure?"

"I'm sure." Ben glanced over the boy's head to his parents. They looked old and tired, completely at a loss as to what to do next. "Whatever we decide regarding Tyler, I want all of you to know that I love him and I want to raise him as my own. And right now, I only want him to be well again. Will you pray with me, for your son and for Tyler?"

Mary bobbed her head, then dabbed at her eyes. Lifting her gaze to her husband, she sent him a pleading look. "Richard, please. God has been so good to our family and now, He's brought our son home and given us the gift of a grandchild, too. Please pray with us."

Richard sat still for a moment, his expression grim, his lips set in a tight line. But finally he reached out a shaky hand to his wife. "I don't know...how to deal with this. Mary, help me. Help me, please."

Tears fell down Mary's cheeks as she took her husband's hand in hers, then turned to her son to grasp his hand on the other side. "With God's help, we'll make it through this, Richard. You know that in your heart. Jason is a good boy, and he's home now. Whatever led him to this, we now have a chance to make things better between us."

He nodded, then cast a hard glance at his son. "Jason, you've made some harsh accusations toward me here today. Son, I never realized how much I've hurt you and I'm sorry. I always did what I thought was best. I worked hard to provide for my family and I tried to raise all of my children with the proper values and in the Erickson tradition. I don't know where we went wrong, but...I am glad you're home again."

Jason bobbed his head, unable to speak. Ben took his hand as they formed a circle around the table, then he reached out a hand to Richard Erickson. "Let's pray."

Reluctantly Richard took the hand Ben offered and silently lowered his head. Then suddenly he glanced up. "Wait, Reverend."

Ben held his breath, wondering what Richard Erickson would demand now. "Yes?"

Richard's eyes filled with tears. "After we pray...could we please see our grandson?"

Ben had to swallow back his own tears. "Of course."

It was a start. Ben lifted up a prayer of thanksgiving and forgiveness...and hope.

Chapter Sixteen

"Wow. I never would have dreamed in a million years that Tyler belongs to Jason Erickson."

Betty Sinclair shook her head, then glanced around at the group of teachers she'd assembled for the weekly staff meeting. "The Lord sure does work in mysterious ways."

Sara took a sip of her hot tea, then nodded. "And let's hope that the Ericksons consent to this adoption. They could really make things ugly for Ben, if they put their minds to it. So far, though, they've been very cooperative. They've visited Tyler at the hospital almost every day."

Maggie leaned forward in her chair. "Ben told me they're going to counseling with Jason. That should help them get through this rough spot. Maybe Richard will finally soften up toward his son a little when he realizes the rest of us aren't going to turn away from any of them."

Betty checked her notes, then looked up. "No, they need us now more than ever. I think that man's realized he could lose Jason forever, if he doesn't at least make an effort to change his harsh, condemning nature. Richard is a good man, just a bit too controlling. We're just going to have to pray really hard that he's learned a thing or two about turning control over to God, and we're going to have to show him by example that we can forgive and lend our support to his family during this crisis."

Sara spoke up again. "Jason is adamant about Ben adopting Tyler, so I don't think there will be a problem. Ben hopes to set up some sort of visitation rights with the Ericksons, since they are the baby's grandparents. He told me about it last night at the hospital."

"That is good news," Betty replied. Then getting down to business, she added, "And we're thrilled to announce that all of our children have been checked out thoroughly—no signs of meningitis. Seems the precautionary medicine and all of our disinfecting efforts have paid off."

Julianne breathed a sigh of relief. "Does that mean I can come back to work now?"

"Yes." Betty beamed a smile toward her. "You and your pregnancy are safe. And Tyler is on the mend. Just got a report from Sara regarding that cutie-pie."

Sadie, who'd been asked to sit in on the meeting since she'd been substituting so much lately, laughed a throaty chuckle and gave Sara a big-eyed smile. "And what else does Miss Sara have to report?"

"That's about it," Sara told the group. "As you all know, I'll be leaving at the end of the week."

"Right before Christmas?" Sadie looked crestfallen. "You'll miss the bazaar and...you have to stay for the Christmas Eve service."

"I don't know—"

"She's being stubborn," Maggie interjected, nudging Sara with her elbow.

"I'm being practical," Sara replied, uncomfortable with this whole business. "Can we get on with the official meeting?"

"Testy today, aren't we?" But Betty took the hint and started going over the schedule.

Which gave Sara time to think about the last few days. After Jason had announced that he was Tyler's father, things had come to a standstill for Ben and Sara while they concentrated all their efforts and energy on seeing Tyler through his sickness, and helping Jason to get back in his father's good graces. Thankfully the baby had pulled through like a trooper and was now headed toward a full recovery. And Jason was home for good, coping, and visiting Tyler every day.

But where would Tyler wind up? And where did that leave Sara's relationship with Ben? He was worried; she could tell that. She'd relieved him at the hospital, taking the afternoon and early-evening shifts so he could catch up on his work. But they'd had little time for any personal conversations, what with the constant interruptions by doctors and nurses, and well-meaning, concerned friends.

Maybe that was just as well. Maybe the best thing she could do now was go, before she opened her heart up to another rejection. Ben would be just fine. He'd have Tyler.

And she'd be left with nothing, no one. She'd waited, hoping Ben would talk to her, ask her how she felt about his marriage proposal. But she'd given him an answer already, in no uncertain terms. Why should he ask her again? He had no way of knowing she'd had a change of heart, after all.

"Don't polish that shiny stone into a hollowed-out hole," Sadie told her, her dark eyes full of compassion and understanding.

Sara hadn't even realized she'd been clutching her cross necklace. Quickly dropping her hand, she said, "I've got a lot on my mind. Sorry."

"Don't apologize," Sadie said. "You're going to be okay, Miss Sara Conroy."

"You're sure about that, huh?"

"Very sure." Sadie touched a finger to Sara's necklace. "He's watching over you."

Confused, Sara asked, "God, you mean?"

"God, and Ben Hunter," Sadie replied, then chuckled. "And let me tell you something, sister, that is one mighty powerful combination."

A few days later, Sara remembered Sadie's words to her.

One mighty powerful combination.

That was so true.

Until she'd come here and met Ben and found her faith again, Sara hadn't had anything powerful in her life. Oh, she'd had her work, but it had consumed most of her energy, leaving little time for her own nourishment of the soul. And she'd had her mother, but her mother's illness had taken over that relationship. She'd had Steven, but their commitment hadn't been strong enough to survive anything more than a day-to-day existence. And throughout all of it, Sara had thought she'd been in control.

But she hadn't been. She'd only been half-alive, going through the process, doing her duty. She hadn't really been living. Until now.

No, Sara hadn't known the power or the joy of love until she'd found Ben, and Tyler, and God.

Or as Ben had told her, God had found her.

Only, now it was Christmas Eve and she'd be leaving soon. She'd agreed to spend Christmas with Maggie and her family, only because she couldn't bear to spend that special day alone in the city. With Tyler well and out of the hospital, there was really no reason for Sara to hang around after the holidays, but oh, how she dreaded leaving.

Now as she stood looking at several half-filled boxes, torn between packing them and unpacking them, she wondered if she'd have the strength to attend the Christmas Eve services a couple of hours from now. It might be the last time she'd ever see Ben or Tyler.

All week long, she'd waited, hoping Ben would come to her, talk with her. He'd said they had some things to discuss. Had he had a change of heart? Had he decided he no longer wanted her in his life?

Sara automatically headed toward the windows so she could watch the wintry dusk fall like a velvety blanket over the white woods surrounding the lake. A soft snowfall rained down on the forest, reminding Sara of glistening frozen tears. It was a beautiful, peaceful night. A silent night.

Sara stood there, listening to the silence, her heart opening to God's grace. "Help me," she whispered. "Show me what to do next."

She waited, wondering if God sent signs or announced His grand plans. But the silence continued.

And in that silence Sara thought back over her life, searching, hoping, until at last she found her answers.

At last she understood completely.

Turning back to her boxes, she set about her work.

Ben checked his watch, then turned in the car to make sure Tyler was snug in his seat. He was so glad the baby had been released from the hospital a few days ago with a clean bill of health.

And just in time to spend his first Christmas at home, with Ben.

"Hope we make it, little fellow," Ben told the baby.

In a little over an hour or so, he had to deliver the Christmas Eve sermon. Not too much time, but he'd make it if he hurried. Only, he didn't want to hurry in this. It had to be right this time.

Pulling the vehicle up close to Sara's door, Ben ran around to get Tyler, making sure the baby was well protected from the delicate snowflakes falling all around them. It was Tyler's first outing since coming home, and although the doctors had assured Ben the baby was completely well, he didn't want to take any chances.

But he had to see Sara.

Such a beautiful night. So still and silent. It was as if the whole night was waiting, waiting for the miracle of Christmas.

Ben wanted to spend this night with those he loved the most in life—Sara and Tyler.

"It's now or never, son," he told Tyler as he cuddled the baby close. Tyler gurgled and cooed his agreement.

Taking that as a sign of encouragement, Ben knocked on the door.

Sara heard the knock, and startled, dropped the bundle of clothes she'd had in her hands. When she opened the door and saw Ben standing there with Tyler in his arms, a fierce joy lifted her heart to a gentle humming.

"Come in." Touching a hand to Tyler's cap, she

blinked back tears. "Oh, Ben. He looks so rested and well. I'm so glad."

"Me, too. We wanted you to be the first to see that he's healthy and happy again."

Sara took Tyler from him, hugging the baby close to enjoy the scent of baby powder mixed with Ben's distinctive spicy aftershave. "Tyler, I'm so glad you're all better."

Turning to Ben, she motioned him inside the room. "So what brings you two out to the lake? I thought you'd be getting ready for the main event."

"We came to ask you to ride to the church with us." Ben's happy expression immediately changed as he glanced around the room, the smile on his face slicing into a frown. "Have we interrupted your packing?"

Sara's gaze flew to his face. "Ben, I—"

Ben held up a hand. "Sara, before you tell me that you're leaving Fairweather, I think there are a few things we need to get straight."

"All right, but—"

"Please?" Ben interrupted with the same hand, held even higher. "I really need to talk to you."

She motioned to the couch, afraid to say anything more. "Let's sit down, then."

After getting Tyler settled between them with a rattle, she offered Ben something to drink. But he refused. The serious look on his face didn't give Sara much hope.

"What's wrong, Ben?"

"Everything," he said, his voice so soft she had

to strain toward him. "I messed up big-time, Sara. But I'm here to make things right."

"Oh?" Hope was back, bright and shining.

Ben gave Tyler a lopsided smile, then looked at her, his eyes so open and honest she wanted to cry.

"I never told you about Nancy, did I?"

Sara shook her head, suddenly realizing that the secret she'd longed to hear from his own lips no longer mattered. "Everyone else did, but not you."

He nodded slowly, understanding dawning in his eyes. "And you never questioned that?"

"I felt you'd tell me when the time was right. At least that's what I hoped."

He reached across Tyler to take her hand in his. "The time is right. I loved Nancy with all my heart."

"I know," she said, dreading his next words. "I understand, Ben. Really, I do."

"I think you do," he replied, his hand squeezing hers. "But I've been so unfair to you. I loved Nancy so much, I thought I would dishonor that love if I gave in to my feelings for you."

"I know," she repeated, bracing herself for the pain of his rejection.

She didn't want to hear him say that he would never be able to love anyone else. So she decided to say what was in her heart, simply because she had reached the point of no return. She had no other choice, no other options. She was going to see this through, and she wouldn't give up without at least being honest.

Sara held his hand tight to hers, taking that final leap of faith. "But I love you anyway."

The look of surprise on Ben's face was classic. He looked both relieved and confused, and completely lost. "You do?"

"Yes, Ben. I love you. I loved you when you asked me to marry you, and that's why I turned you down."

He also looked dazed and defeated. "Okay. So you love me, but you can't marry me? Is that why you're packing to leave?"

Sara looked around at the boxes, half empty, half full, depending, she supposed, on how you looked at things. "No, that's why I'm *unpacking*. I decided just a little while ago to stay and...fight for our love. I realized that I've always given up on things too soon. I gave up on my work because the hospital insisted I needed to, I gave up on Steven because he gave up on me, and I gave up on my mother, because I got too tired to fight her disease. But I'm not going to give up on you and Tyler. I love you, Ben."

The smile on Ben's face told her everything she needed to know. With a shaky chuckle, he said, "So...if I were to get down on my knee—" he did just that "—and present you with this ring—" he pulled out a black velvet box and opened it to reveal a small, perfectly rounded diamond. "This time you'd agree to marry me?"

Sara gasped, her hand going to her cross necklace, her eyes brimming with tears. "Yes, I would.

I would agree to marry you, to love you always, to be a mother to Tyler, to be the best preacher's wife I can be. I'd agree to just about anything, as long as you'd offer to love me.''

Ben reached for her hand, then placed the ring on her finger. "I'm offering, then. I love you, Sara. And I loved you the night I asked you to marry me—the first time."

"You did?"

"Yes, I did. I had to work through a lot of things in order to reach that conclusion, but in the end, my love for you won out over all my doubts and my guilt about Nancy. I was just too afraid to tell you that then."

"Oh, Ben. What took you so long?"

Tyler let out a string of gurgles then, his eyes bright with the innocence of a child as he focused on something outside, beyond the long row of windows.

They both turned to see a brightly lit star shining off the dock across the lake.

"It's our star," Ben told her, his voice low and gravelly. "From the restaurant, remember?"

"I remember," Sara replied. "It's the Christmas star. They turn it on every night at dusk."

Ben leaned over to kiss Tyler, then he kissed his future wife. "'And a little child shall lead them.'"

Sara smiled as she pulled him to her. "I'm so glad God found me and brought me to Fairweather."

Epilogue

Ben stood at the altar with Sara, both of them smiling down at the eight-month-old baby they'd officially adopted a week earlier. The week before that, they'd said their marriage vows right here in The Old First Church, in a beautiful springtime wedding, with both Reverend Olsen and Reverend Winslow officiating.

Both reverends were back today, too. Because on this Easter Sunday, Tyler was being christened. And all around him were the people who would promise to be examples in his life, to guide him, love him, cherish him in God's holy name.

That included Richard and Mary Erickson and their son, Jason. Jason was back in school now, with tutoring from Ben and several other church members to help him catch up on his grades. He'd soon be looking toward college.

The adoption had gone through without any problems or disputes. The Ericksons had visitation privileges with Tyler, and that included Jason. Ben didn't know what the future would bring, but if Jason one day decided to tell Tyler that he was his biological father, Ben would back him and trust that God would guide them through it.

Patty was back in school, too, and still living with her sister. She'd kept her promise and signed the papers without question. She told Ben that she loved Tyler enough to give him to someone who could love him and help him grow and flourish. Tyler had changed her life, and now she was working hard to make that life better, and she was encouraging her mother to seek help, too.

Ben thanked God that he now had Sara and Tyler in his life. They were a family at last and settled into a routine with Sara working part-time at the hospital and Ben getting back full-time to his own job, and Tyler being spoiled with love from all quarters. But today brought yet another blessing to their joining.

Ben listened as the christening ceremony continued. Maggie and Frank had agreed to be Ben's godparents, and the rest of the congregation now pledged to watch over the baby and teach him in the ways of Christ.

After the ministers sprinkled Tyler's head with holy water, Reverend Winslow handed Tyler over to Ben, then stood back with his own bride of one month, Alice, to admire their new grandson.

"Show him to the people," he told Ben, urging him around.

Ben grinned, then took Tyler in his arms to walk out into the congregation while Sara beamed and wiped tears from her eyes.

"Everyone, I'd like you to meet our son, Jason Tyler Erickson Hunter," Ben said, pride evident in the words.

Then he walked back to Sara, leaning over to kiss her on the cheek. Tyler, tiring of all this fuss, and eager to go back into his mother's arms, let out a yell of protest at being ignored while Mommy stared lovingly into Daddy's eyes.

As everyone laughed, Ben handed the baby to Sara, then headed to the podium to deliver the Easter sermon, his heart full, his faith overflowing.

"That's our Tyler," he told the congregation. "He's our little bundle of joy. And what better way to begin the topic of today's sermon. It's about another little boy, born a very long time ago...."

* * * * *

If you enjoyed reading

BEN'S BUNDLE OF JOY,

*you'll love Lenora Worth's next book
from Steeple Hill Love Inspired...*

THE RELUCTANT HERO

*Ambitious reporter Stephanie Maguire
stumbles onto Derek Kane's
heroic deeds and vows to uncover
his dark secret. But the more time she
spends with him, the more
she realizes that she has to make
a choice between her story and her
love for this reluctant hero.*

*Don't miss it!
On sale July 2000
ISBN: 0-373-87114-7*

Dear Reader,

Being a part of this series was such a joy for me. At first it was hard bringing to life characters that someone else had created, but the more involved I became with Ben and Sara and little Tyler, the more fun I had.

I learned so much from this story and these characters. Being a Christian sometimes means that others think of us as picture perfect, almost above reproach. But we're not. We're just humans who struggle every day with right and wrong, good and bad, grief and joy. But we know that we have someone to turn to, in the good times and the bad.

Sara learned that lesson when she saw just how much she'd been missing without God's guidance in her life, and Ben had to remember that not only was he a minister to serve God and others, but he had to also minister to himself. They both stepped out of the darkness and into the light, and together they found their joy. I hope this story brings you a little bit of lightness and joy.

Until next time, may the angels watch over you while you sleep.

Lenora Worth